Also by Joseph O'Neill

Good Trouble

Good Trouble

◇◇◇

Stories

Joseph O'Neill

Pantheon Books, New York

Copyright © 2018 by Joseph O'Neill

All rights reserved. Published in the United States by Pantheon Books, a division of Penguin Random House LLC, New York, and distributed in Canada by Random House of Canada, a division of Penguin Random House Canada Limited, Toronto.

Pantheon Books and colophon are registered trademarks of Penguin Random House LLC.

Owing to limitations of space, information on previously published material appears on page 159.

Library of Congress Cataloging-in-Publication Data
Name: O'Neill, Joseph, [date] author.
Title: Good trouble : stories / Joseph O'Neill.
Description: First edition. New York : Pantheon Books, [2018]
Identifiers: LCCN 2017040305. ISBN 9781524747350 (hardcover : acid-free paper). ISBN 9781524747367 (ebook)
Classification: LCC PR6065.N435 A6 2018. DDC 823/.914—dc23.
LC record available at lccn.loc.gov/2017040305

www.pantheonbooks.com

Jacket illustration by Belhassen Chtioui
Jacket design by Janet Hansen

Printed in the United States of America
First Edition
2 4 6 8 9 7 5 3 1

To Gill Coleridge and to David McCormick

Contents

Good Trouble

Pardon Edward Snowden

◇

The poet Mark McCain received an e-mail, which had been sent to numerous American poets, inviting him to sign a "petition" requesting President Barack H. Obama to pardon Edward Snowden. The request took the form of a poem written by Merrill Jensen, a writer whom Mark knew to be twenty-eight years old, a full nine years his junior. The poem-petition rhymed "Snowden" with "pardon." And "pardon" with "Rose Garden." And "Rose Garden" with "nation." And "nation" with "Eden." It rhymed—or, as Mark preferred to put it, it echoed—"Putin" and "boot in" and "Clinton" and "no disputing." "Russia" echoed "USA"; and "USA" "Thoreau"; and "Thoreau" "hero."

Mark forwarded the e-mail to the poet E. W. West. He wrote:

Am I crazy to find this enraging?

Within seconds Liz wrote back:

No.

They arranged to have coffee that afternoon.

◇

In preparation for the meeting, Mark tried to organize his thoughts. His first point, of course, was that the very idea of poem as petition was misconceived. A poem was first and last a *Ding an sich*. It definitely wasn't a message that boiled down to a single political-humanitarian demand. It made no sense for an agreeing multitude, or mob, to undersign a poem: you could no more agree with a poem than with a tree, even if you'd written it. Of course, the signers of the poetition would argue that they were associating themselves with the text's petitionary substance and not with its formal properties; and that in any case poetry is a sword of lightning that consumes its scabbard. But, accepting all that, Mark mentally counterclaimed, why not just have a petition in the form of a petition? Why drag the poem into the muck? Because, the undersigned might reply, a versified petition was likely to attract more attention and be more consequential than the alternative. To which Mark would answer, The good of poetry resides not in the—

He began to feel a familiar dialectical dizziness. He set off to meet his friend, even though it meant that he would get there twenty minutes early.

Liz was waiting for him when he arrived.

They hugged. The moment they took their seats, Liz said, "Well, are you going to sign it?"

Mark said, "I don't know. Are you?"

Liz said, "Not my problem. Nobody's asked me to."

Mark paused. This was a complexity he ought to have foreseen. With extravagant bitterness, he said, "Oh, they'll rope you in."

Liz mused, "I did a reading with Merrill in January."

Mark had attended the event, as Liz well knew. "I felt bad for him," he told her. "You really showed him up. Without meaning to, of course." He went on, "Look, I do think this thing is chaotic. They're basically shooting out e-mails at random. And I don't think Merrill is a vengeful, petty guy. Far from it. I think his heart's in the right place. Ish. But you know what? I could be wrong. He's obviously interested in a certain kind of success." Mark stopped there and was glad he had, even though he loathed Merrill Jensen. Whenever he bad-mouthed a colleague, however justifiably, he regretted it. (Strange, just how draining an effort of tact was required to get through the day without bad-mouthing another poet.) In this instance, he felt, he hadn't thrown Merrill Jensen under the bus. He'd dissed him only in order to express solidarity with Liz, and only to that extent.

Liz doubted that Merrill had overlooked her because she'd shown him up at their reading; in all probability, Merrill's recollection was that he'd shown *her* up. No, she had been overlooked because she was a woman. Whenever a stand needed to be taken and the attention of the public had to be endured, the peacocks huffed and squawked to the fore, idiotically iridescent.

She decided to say, "We need people like Merrill. Somebody's got to be interested in being prominent. Otherwise we'd all disappear."

Mark said, "I expect Dylan has been contacted."

Liz laughed. The singer's Nobel Prize in Literature had bothered her, yes. Literature was in the first place reading matter, after all, and Dylan's lyrics were mostly unreadable—and not even listenable to without the music. Even his supposedly best stuff would be torn apart if presented to the poetry practicum she taught every Tuesday, not only on account of its wordy, clichéd, hyperactive figuration but, more fundamentally, because of the soothsaying persona that the singer so readily deployed, a move that worked fine in a pop song but on paper came off as a shtick. All that said, Liz had not taken the news as a personal hit. Mark, though, in common with many men of the pen she knew, had been knocked flat. For two days he could not bring himself to leave his apartment or even to post on Facebook. Only after this period of grieving had he managed to discuss the matter with Liz, at the very table where they now sat. At that meeting, Mark revealed that the night before he'd found himself thinking back to the seventeen-year-old who, wandering the public library of Forsyth, Missouri, inexplicably leafed through a tattered *Norton Anthology* and for the first time came truly face-to-face with a poem's mysterious verb-visage. He still remembered the one that did it for him—Roethke's "The Waking," funnily enough. *So take the lively air, / And, lovely, learn by going where to go,* he recited to Liz. And that was the moment he'd set off on a delightful clueless journey in language, and for years he never once felt lonely or even singular, because at all times he felt this breeze, he said to Liz, on which the poems he would read and write might be accepted and held firmly aloft, and the air of the culture seemed filled with such breezes and such poems. Yes, Liz said, I know exactly what you mean. Frank O'Hara did it for me, she said. Which one? Mark asked. Liz said, "Animals," to which Mark replied, *We didn't need speedometers / we could manage cocktails out of ice and water,* and Liz wanted to hug her friend. Anyhow, Mark continued, the damn thing is, it's so hard to keep believing. And there's so much you need to believe in. Does that make sense to you? It does, Liz said. Mark said, You become aware that what you're doing is almost nothing. That it's just a few atoms away from nothing. And now, with this scandal, I feel that what we do is in fact nothing. I feel like it's officially nothing. Liz saw that Mark had other things he'd planned to say but was too emotional to speak. Liz, they're calling him a poet, he finally got out. You know? They're not calling him a novelist. They're not calling him a songwriter. They're saying he's a poet, Liz. I know, sweetie, Liz had said.

"Seems like he's finally accepted the honor," she now stated.

Mark said, "Of course he accepted it. A guy with that much vanity! He was always going to accept it."

He didn't tell Liz that, during the couple of weeks that Dylan had not responded to the news of his award, Mark had hoped that the singer would tell the Swedish buffoons where to stick it; that Bob had the integrity to recognize that an ultra-celebrated multimillionaire who deals in concerts and extra-paginal iconicity is not playing the same game as a writer who sits down in a small college town and, with no prospect of meaningful financial reward, tries to come up with a handful of words that will, unless something untoward should happen, be read by a maximum of a hundred and forty people and be properly appreciated by maybe fifty-two of these, of whom maybe six will be influenced. Make that two. Once a year a small beam of honor, reflected all the way from Stockholm, faintly brightened the dim endeavors of such writers. And now even this glimmer had been removed from their small and dark corner of the sky

and tossed like a trinket into Bob Dylan's personal con-
stellation.

This sidereal imagery made Mark uneasy—stars were
almost always cheesy; doubly cheesy, in the context of
a "pop star"—but he had nothing else. Language was
hard. And poetry, he'd always felt, was language at its
hardest.

He had recently expressed this point of view to his
friend Jarvis, a writer of short-form fiction. Jarvis said,
"Really? Poetry is hard, sure. But good prose is just as
hard, man."

"Poets can generally do what prose writers do,"
Mark, a little drunk, declared. "The reverse? Not so
much."

A day later, he received an e-mail from Jarvis with a
poem attached:

Easy Peasy

It seems that what's
Keeping what is as it is, the whole thing thing,
    is physics, whatever
That is. Let's see: the fizz of the river, *l'hiver,*
    that Swiss
Watch thing. Liver.
Every frisson, everything that's
Alive or that was once aliver. The leaf. The leaver.

He forwarded it to Liz:

What do you think?

She wrote back:

So great that you're writing again! This is good—
best thing you've done in a while. So effortless.
"Physics" and "fizz" is a pleasure. And don't
think I haven't noticed that the English-language
contractions erase "i" and "u." In a poem drown-
ing in materialism, that's just such a smart, play-
ful way to raise the issue of subjectivity.

Mark didn't get back to Liz. Or to Jarvis.
Re the Dylan Nobel, Liz said, "It's depressing. I can't
separate it from the Trump phenomenon."
The election was a week away.
"Yes," Mark said. "And hypercapitalism, too. The
reader as consumer. It's an interesting question."

He kept secret, even from Liz, the fact that he'd already
written on this question. It was a secret because what
he'd written wasn't a poem. For some months, Mark
had worked surreptitiously, and exclusively, on a series
of prose reflections that he termed "pensées."

How doable pensées were! The most difficult thing
about making a poem, in Mark's judgment, was figur-
ing out the text's relation to its own knowledge; figur-
ing out, to quote from Liz's one anthologized work, the
poem's "claim to saying." There was no such problem
with a pensée: you wrote as a know-all. Apparently—
and here, Nietzsche and Cioran and above all Adorno
were Mark's masters—the trick was to simply put to one
side all epistemological difficulties and just steam ahead
into the realm of assertion and opinion and emphasis.
Boy, it felt good. With great gusto Mark had knocked
out, apropos of the hypercapitalistic reader:

As class-based *submissiveness* justly evaporates, appropriate *deference*—to expertise, rationality, and even data—also disappears.

This results from a state of affairs in which one's autonomy consists primarily in a freedom to consume. Objective realities are inspected like supermarket apples and accepted only if they tickle the fancy. If they don't, it's not sufficient merely to reject the apple. The apple tree itself must be cut down. And then the orchard. Hell hath no fury like a consumer inconvenienced.

In this way, shopping is confused with resistance; a bogus egalitarianism prevails; a vicious man-on-the-streetism becomes dominant. The *tricoteuses* make their return, clicking not needles but touchpads. Need one add that the poem is the first to be dragged to the guillotine?

Who knew that writing this stuff would be such fun? The voice—at once pedantic and forceful, and strangely aged and pampered—was the most fun of all. It was the voice of the short-tempered Central European professor whose wife's principal domestic project is to ensure that her husband enjoys peace and quiet in his study.

Mark had not had a wife or a study in six years. Liz and he became close during the chaos of his divorce, when he was outed as a cuckold and outed from his house. His male friends, he was a little shocked to learn, were ineffectual, indiscreet, and bizarrely merciless confidants. Liz listened to him sympathetically—and honestly, too. When Mark said to her, I was blindsided, Liz said, Yeah, maybe, and he said, What do you mean, maybe? and Liz said, Quarterbacks are blindsided. You weren't blindsided. You were myopic.

Liz's criticism of Mark's poetry was similarly sensitive and forthright, and he was very grateful for it and happy to reciprocate. Her work wasn't right up his alley—it was a little too academic and sexual—but there was no querying its intelligence and carefulness. In any case, Mark mistrusted his own alley, which at this point, as he'd once remarked to Liz, was overrun by the rats of resentment. And the cats of confusion, Liz suggested. Not to mention the dogs of disillusionment.

If Mark envied Liz at all, it was for the growing kudos that E. W. West enjoyed as a writer who disturbed edifices of gender and sexuality. But it wasn't Liz's fault that her biologically and culturally determined homoerotic inclinations were now in vogue, just as it could hardly be held against her that she'd grown up in bourgeois luxury on the Upper West Side of Manhattan. (Liz often complained to Mark about finding herself in Virginia, a dislocation that she experienced, as any reader of her "Sappho in Sicily" quickly grasped, as an exile.) Nor did he hold it against Liz that, in an unpublicized complication of her biographical profile, she was for the first time romantically involved with a man. His name was Pickett, apparently as a tribute to Wilson Pickett. Did anyone call their children after poets anymore? Mark doubted that there'd ever be a kid named McCain out there in the world. Or, if there would, the kid would certainly be named for the political weasel John McCain. Mark had long felt defamed by this echo.

Every word is a prejudice, Nietzsche famously points out. One might add: Every word *prejudices*. Nowhere is this truer than in the nominal realm. One's name cannot be separated from one's good name.

He cared deeply for Liz and was her biggest fan and cheerleader. He felt bad that she had not been contacted about the Snowden poetition.

"So what should I do?" he asked her. "Sign it? Rewrite it?"

"Ah," Liz said. "The patriarch's quandary."

Mark did the work of smiling sympathetically. He saw that Liz was peeved, and hurt, and with good cause. The problematic situation of women was not to be underestimated, not that Liz was in danger of committing this error. In her most recent sonnet, "mandate" had been displaced by the neologism "womandate." Now Liz was, as she liked to say, lady-pissed. Mark totally got it.

But in the meantime he had a problem of his own, and an itch to explore the problem in writing. They had finished their coffees and their refills. It was time to go.

The two friends stepped outside. It was a lovely November afternoon. They hugged and separately went off.

As soon as he got back to his apartment, he wrote:

We attribute to Bertrand Russell the following notion, that to acquire immunity from eloquence is of utmost importance for citizens of a democracy. We are curious about the notion because Stevens was. And we connect Russell's statement, thanks to Denis Donoghue, to this one, by Locke: "I cannot but observe how little the preservation and improvement of truth and knowledge is the care and concern of mankind, since the arts of fallacy are endowed and preferred."

If we grant Russell's words a merely provisional

validity, we can ask: What is a verse petition if not fallacious eloquence? What is poetry if not a riposte to the forces of fallaciousness? What are these forces if not power's language?

Mark wondered if he should explain that, by "fallacy," Locke meant "deception." He decided not to. The reader would connect the dots.

Not for the first time, Mark asked himself who this notional reader was. He had never, not once, met a disinterested party who had even heard of his poetry, never mind read any of it. Maybe his pensées would gain him a reader he could physically touch.

He felt a wavelet of nausea. The feeling had a certain etymological justice. He had jumped from one ship to another. But what was the alternative? To write nothing? It had been months since he'd produced, or even wanted to produce, a word of poetry.

Mark wrote:

How little I associate writing, properly undertaken, with the generation of the written. The more someone writes, the more suspicious I am of his credentials—as if this person had neglected his actual vocation in favor of the meretricious enterprise of putting words on the page.

Then:

Sometimes I sit down to write and feel the internal presence of . . . bad faith. Therefore I desist from writing. On the other hand, what would it mean to write in good faith? That sounds even more suspect.

He ate a cheese sandwich with mustard and olive oil. That was dinner. He went to his armchair. He wrote:

It is assumed that the writer's first allegiance is to language. This is false. The writer's first allegiance is to silence.

Now it was dark out. Usually the poet would read a book, but tonight he lacked the wherewithal. He opened a can of beer and went online. For a while he skipped from one site to another. Everything was either about the election or not about the election. He checked his e-mail. Nothing new. Then he went onto Facebook, then back to skipping around the Internet. He found himself reading, without interest but with close attention, about persimmon farmers in Florida. He rechecked his e-mail. Hello, Merrill had written him again.

Actually, Merrill had written Merrill—Mark had been bcc'd. The e-mail brought "exciting news": funding had been secured (from whom, Merrill didn't say) to buy half a page in the *Times* for the poetition. This moves the needle, Merrill stated.

Mark's reaction involved three thoughts. One: "Move the needle"? Two: What an operator Merrill Jensen was. What a maestro of fallacy. Mark knew for a fact that Merrill not only disliked Bob Dylan's lyrics but also disliked Bob Dylan's songs, which he'd once sneeringly characterized to Mark, who did like them, as "Pops' music." But sure enough, the minute the Nobel was announced, the prick was at the forefront of the congratulators and imprimatur-givers, arguing that Bob Dylan was an unacknowledged legislator of the world; ergo, Bob Dylan was a poet. It made Mark want to puke: the pseudo-reasoning, so right-wing in its dishonesty; and the big lie that Dylan somehow lacked acknowledgment. The big truth, not that anyone dared to speak it, was that Shelley's dictum needed to be revised. Poets were the unacknowledged poets of the world.

Had Mark been among the scores of writers contacted by the media for their reaction to the prize—which he hadn't been—he would have spoken up for his comrades in verse. He would have faced down the wrathful online barbarians who vilified any perceived anti-Dylanite. (Their favorite disparagement, tellingly, was to accuse one of being a "nobody.") He would have stated:

> The status of poet is not to be worn like one of those fine ceremonial gowns sported by recipients of honorary degrees for a single, sunny, glorious afternoon. Not even by Bob Dylan. If there is such a thing as a poet's mantle, it is a $4.99 plastic poncho: useless for fashion but good in the rain and the cold. And in an emergency.

His third thought about Merrill's e-mail was that his name had never appeared in the *Times* and that if he signed the poetition it would.

His apartment was on the third floor of a Victorian only minimally maintained by its owner. There was a bedroom and a kitchen–living room equipped with an armchair, a desk, a desk lamp, a small sofa, and book-cases that entirely covered two walls. No television. The kitchen-living room had two windows. When Mark wanted to pace about the apartment, his one option was to walk to and from these windows. This he now did.

It was a journey that he'd made thousands of times, and thousands of times he had viewed the shingled rooftops of the houses across the street, and beyond them, in the town's small business district, two brown glassy towers. At night, you couldn't see much beyond the glare of the streetlight directly in front of the window. And yet evidently there was an inextinguishable need to approach an opening built into a wall for air and light, and to look through it.

Somebody down there was walking a dog. That was a poem, right there: the master, the leash, the joyful dog, etc. But the territory had been covered. There was that Nemerov poem, just for starters; and the one by Heather McHugh with that all-time-great dog line—*doctor of crotches*. A poem by Mark McCain would be water poured into a vessel that was already full: superfluous.

He kept looking, which was another poem—a poem about the peculiar percipience of the one who gazes out a window. The poem would do for the window what theorists had done for the threshold: it would offer the idea of the fenestral as a consort to the idea of the liminal. He wouldn't write it. The automatic metaphoric associativity of "the window" was just too much. He could always play with the associations, of course. But surely there had to be better things to do than play with the associations of "the window."

He returned to his chair and wrote, in less than half an hour, a poem that deviated from his previous work. The poem masqueraded as notes for a possible poem. It was titled "Meditation on What It Means to Write?" It read:

Problem: "meditation on" is a cliché. "What it
    means to" is a cliché.
The very notion of a problem, colon, is a cliché.
"The very notion of" is a cliché.
"Cliché" strikes one as a cliché.
As does "strikes one."
And "As does."
Ditto inverted commas.
Ditto "ditto."

He did not write Merrill back. He did not put his
name to the poetition.

As soon as he had not done these things, he rose up
from his chair. He went not to the window but to the
area between the chair and sofa. He stood there with
hands balled into shaking fists. Silently and exultantly he
roared, Never give in. Never not resist.

The Trusted Traveler

◇

For almost a decade, Chris and I have received an annual
visit from one of my former students, Jack Bail. This year
is different. When, as usual, he e-mails to invite himself
over, I reply that "our traditional dinner" can "alas" no
longer take place: six months ago, Christine and I moved
to Nova Scotia.

Jack Bail writes back:

> Nova Scotia? Canada's Ocean Playground? I'm
> there, Doc. Just say when and where.

"Oh no," Chris says. "I'm so sorry, love."

It's I who should say sorry to Chris. Not only will
she have to cook for Jack Bail but she will also have to
handle Jack Bail, because, even though I'm supposedly
the one who's Jack Bail's friend, it's Chris who retains
the details of Jack Bail's life story and the details of what
transpired in the course of our meals with him, and who
is able to follow what Jack Bail is saying or feeling. For
some reason, almost anything that has to do with Jack

Bail is beyond my grasp. I can't even remember having taught anybody named Jack Bail.

"And I guess Chris will be coming," Chris says, confusingly. "His wife," Chris says.

Of course—Jack Bail's wife, like my Chris, is a Chris by way of Christine. Which is irritating.

I say, "You never know. Maybe he won't be able to make it."

Chris laughs, as well she might. Jack Bail always turns up. Without fail he marks the end of the tax season by eating at our table. It is always a strangely fictional few hours. Only after Jack Bail has left does our life again feel factual.

Chris's long-standing opinion on the Jack Bail situation is that I should effectively communicate to him that I don't wish to see him. It's not her suggestion that I socially fire him in writing—as she acknowledges, "That's pretty much psychologically impossible"—but that I make use of the well-understood convention of e-mail silence.

I've tried it. E-mail silence only prompts Jack Bail to switch to pushy text messages. For example:

> Hi about this dinner thing. Just let me know details as soon as you have them, no rush.

This obdurate memorandum and others like it—

> Dinner this month? Next month? All good :)

—weigh on me so heavily that in the end it's just easier to spend an evening with the guy. The truth isn't so much that Jack Bail is a terrible or unbearable fellow but that Jack Bail falls squarely into the category of people whom Chris and I really don't want to see anymore as we hit our mid-sixties and apprehend the finitude and irreversibility of human time as an all-too-vivid personal actuality and not as a literary theme to be discussed in high school classes devoted to *The Count of Monte Cristo* or *The Old Man and the Sea.* A central purpose of moving to this Canadian coastal hilltop has been to shed our skins as New Yorkers and finally rid ourselves of the purely dutiful associations that, it seemed to me especially, overcrowded our day-to-day existences, which, even discounting work, apparently amounted to one interaction after another with individuals who demanded that we transfer our time to them, often for no better reason than that our paths had once crossed or, would you believe it, that their very demand for our time constituted such a crossing of paths.

(Illustration: A, who claims to be a friend of a friend, informs me by e-mail that he's thinking of applying for a job at the school where Chris and I teach. Could he pick my brains over coffee? Further illustration: B writes to Chris to say that her child once attended the school. Could Chris help B get an overseas research fellowship? Exercising what is, I believe, a universally accepted right to reasonable personal autonomy, we choose not to answer these approaches; whereupon, we find out, both A and B tell people that we're rude, selfish, full of ourselves, etc. In A's and B's minds, their making unilateral contact with us means that we, the contactees, are somehow in their debt. The difference between Chris and me is that she doesn't let this stuff get to her, whereas I stupidly waste a lot of time and emotion being bothered by the ridiculous injustice and hostility of it all.)

I won't even begin to describe how many hours and years we devoted to the parental body—the Hydra, as Chris named it. You cannot defeat the Hydra. You can only flee it. None of this is to say that we're refugees; but it can't be denied that we've retired, and that to retire means to draw back, as if from battle.

The good news is Jack and Chris Bail will not be sleeping over. My Chris took it upon herself to warn Jack Bail and his Chris that there was no room at our inn, so to speak, to which Jack Bail responded:

No worries.

We'll take him at his word. The other good news is that Ed and Fran Joyce, new Nova Scotia acquaintances, will join us for the dinner in order to absorb the Bails, although of course the Joyces aren't aware that this is part of their function. We don't know the Joyces at all well, but they strike us as good sports. Also, they hosted a kind of welcome event for us, and so we owe them dinner, arguably: one day soon after we arrived, a hamper filled with good things was left at our front door, together with an invitation to join members of "the community" for drinks and nibbles. We freely accepted the invitation—we hadn't come here to be recluses, after all—and enjoyed the occasion, although we were, and still are, a little wary of and astonished by and ironical about the prospect of joining a retiree crowd. Our plan is to have a year of contemplative idleness, after which we'll have a better idea of what to next get up to. We're far from elderly, after all. Time is not yet a victorious enemy.

Shortly before everyone is due to turn up, Chris and I take to the deck and get a head start on the wine, which is white and cold. "I wonder what Jack will have to say about this place," Chris says. "Yes," I say. "That's something to look forward to." She has reminded me of Jack Bail's chronic amazement at our old apartment in Hudson Heights. Every time he came over, from Brooklyn, he would say something like, Hudson Heights? Who knew this neighborhood even existed? Who lives up here? Oboe players? It's like I'm in Bucharest or something. Should I buy here?

This kind of thing is all fine, needless to say, and absolutely within my tolerance levels in relation to schoolchildren, although of course Jack Bail, who must be in his late thirties, and if memory serves is balding, is no longer a schoolboy. But his personal qualities are beside the point. The point is that Jack Bail is uncalled-for.

It's a mild, semi-sunny, slightly windy June evening. "Just look at that," I declare for about the millionth time since we moved into our cottage, which offers a panorama of a pond, green seaside hills, a semicircular bay, and a sandbar—or spit, perhaps. To the south, there's a wooded headland that may or may not be a tombolo. It's my intention to investigate this vista systematically, since it feels strange to look out every day and basically not understand what I'm looking at. Right now, for example, I'm observing an extraordinary horizontal triplex: in the offing, a distinctly ultramarine strip of ocean water is topped by a dull-blue band of unclassifiable vapor, itself topped by a purely white stratum of cloud. Then comes sky-blue air and, almost on top of our own hill, an enormous hovering gray cloud. This outlandish hydroatmospheric pileup, which is surely not unknown to science, leaves me at a terminological and informational loss that's only intensified when I look at the bay itself, where the migrant and moody skylight, together with the action of the wind and current, I suppose, and maybe differences in the water's depth and salinity, constantly pattern and texture and streak the aquatic surface. It's unpredictable and beautiful. Sometimes the bay, usually blue or gray, is thoroughly brown, other times it has Caribbean swirls of aquamarine or is colorlessly pale, and invariably there are areas where the water is ruffled, and there are smooth or smoother areas of water, and areas that are relatively dark and light, and dull and brilliant, and so forth, ever more complexly. There must be some field of learning that can help me to better appreciate these phenomena.

"*The Salty Rose*," Chris says. "For the Lunenburg whaling years."

"Not bad at all," I say.

This is one of our favorite running jokes: Chris suggests titles for the memoirs that I am not writing about the lives that we have not led. In this subjunctive world we are adventurers, spies, honorary consuls, nomads, millionaires. *The Hammocks of Chilmark* describes our summers on the Vineyard. Our Corfu stint is the subject of a trilogy: *The Owl in the Jasmine*; *A Pamplemousse for the Captain*; and *Who Shall Water the Bougainvillea?*

We have never set foot on Corfu or Martha's Vineyard. Other than a four-year spell in Athens, Ohio, our thirty-one-year-old marriage and thirty-two-year teaching careers, and almost all of our vacations, have unfolded in and around the schools and streets of New York, New York. Jack Bail claims to have been in my class at Athens High, which is confounding. I have a pretty good recall of those Athens kids.

"Goddamn it."

Chris: "Leg-bug?"

I pick it off my ankle and, because these lentil-sized spider-like little fuckers are tough, I crush and recrush it between the bottom of my glass and my armrest. I call them leg-bugs because these last couple of weeks every time I've set foot outdoors I've caught them crawling up my legs—to what end, I don't know; they're up to no good, you can bet—and because I can't entomologically identify them. They're certainly maddening. Often my shin prickles when there's nothing there.

"Here they are," Chris says.

Our guests have arrived simultaneously, in two cars. Fran and Ed get out of their red pickup and Jack Bail gets out of his rented Hyundai. There's no sign of his Chris.

Dispensing with the steps, Jack Bail strides directly onto the deck. He's extraordinarily tall, maybe six foot six. Has he grown?

"Adirondack chairs," Jack Bail says. "Of course."

As the young visitor who has gone to great lengths, Jack Bail is the object of solicitousness. There's no way around this: once Jack Bail has traveled all the way from New York, he must be received with proportionate hospitality. "Jack first," Fran says, when I try to pour her a glass of wine. "He deserves it, after his voyage."

"The flight was great," Jack Bail says. "Newark

airport—less so." Ed says, "You might want to think about the Trusted Traveler program. Might speed things along." "I am a Trusted Traveler," Jack Bail says. "It did me no good. Not at Newark." "What happens if you're a Trusted Traveler?" Chris says. Ed says, "You don't have to take your shoes off." We all laugh. Jack Bail exclaims, "They made me take my shoes off!" We all laugh again. Ed asks Jack Bail, "Which program you with? NEXUS?" "Global Entry," Jack Bail says. Looking at Fran, Ed says, "That's what I'm all about. Global entry." That gets the biggest, or the politest, laugh of all.

Soon we're eating grilled haddock, asparagus, and field greens. "Delicious," Jack Bail is the first to say. "Thank you, Jack," Chris says, with what seems like real gratitude. Jack Bail inspects the ocean, parts of which are ruddy and other parts dark blue. "That's some view, Doc," Jack Bail says. "Well, it's not Hudson Heights," I say. "I thought you lived in Manhattan?" Fran says. "Hudson Heights is in Manhattan," I say. Ed says, " 'Doc,' eh? You're a dark horse." "That's what they called me," I declare heartily. I didn't invent the custom of recognizing a teacher's academic title. Ed continues, "How about you, Jack? You a doc, too?" Jack laughs. "No way, man. I'm just a CPA." " 'Just'?" Fran says, as if outraged. "You must be very proud of this young man," she tells me, and this is a tiny bit infuriating, because I don't like to receive instruction on how I ought to feel. How proud I am or am not of Jack Bail is for me to decide. "Certainly," I say, Mr. Very Hearty all over again. Fran says, "How was he in the classroom? A rascal, I'll bet." I make a sort of ho-ho-ho, and Jack Bail says to Fran, "Hey, don't blow my cover!" He adds, "Doc was a great teacher." I say, "Well, we've come a long way from Ohio," and Ed says, "We've all come a long way, eh?" and he tells Jack Bail that he's from B.C. but that Fran is a Maritimer and Maritimer women always return home eventually and you'd have to be crazy to stand in the way of a Maritimer woman.

Fran says very attentively, "Your wife can't be with us, Jack?"

"No, Chris is not able to come," Jack Bail says.

"Maybe next time," Fran says. Chris somehow catches my eye without looking at me and somehow rolls her eyes without rolling them. Or so I imagine.

"Unfortunately we're currently separated," Jack Bail says.

This gives everyone pause. "I'm sorry to hear that," Ed says. Jack Bail says, "Yep, it's not an ideal situation."

Now Chris gets up and says, "We have assorted berries, and we have—chocolate cake. Jack's favorite."

"Do you have children, Jack?" Fran asks, which is surely a question whose answer she can figure out by herself. "We don't," Jack Bail says. "A couple of years back, we tried. You know, the IVF thing. Didn't work out." I'm refreshing the tableware at this point. Jack Bail says, "As a matter of fact, I just got this letter from the clinic demanding nine hundred dollars for my sperm."

This silences even the Joyces.

Jack Bail continues, "So three years ago, as part of the whole process, we froze sperm. Yeah, so anyway, we go through the whole thing, an ordeal I guess you could call it, and this and that happens, and we forget all about the frozen sperm. Now here's this invoice for nine hundred bucks because they've stored it all this time—or so they say. I call them up. I speak to a lady. The lady says they've sent letters every year informing me that they're holding my sample. Letters? I don't remember any letters. But first things first, right? Destroy it, I tell her. Get rid of it right away. She tells me that they can't do that. First they need a notarized semen disposition statement."

"OK, here we go," Chris says. "Jack's cake. And berries for anyone who might be interested."

"Now, I know their game," Jack Bail says. "I know what's going to happen. I'm going to mail them the notarized statement and they're going to say they never got it. And they're going to make me go to a notary all over again and they're going to make me mail them another statement and they're going to drag this thing out. And every extra day they store it, they're going to charge more, pro rata. See? They're literally holding my sperm hostage."

"Corporations," Ed says. "Fran, doesn't that—"

"Exactly," Jack Bail says. "It's not that the employees are evildoers. It's the corporate systems. When it comes to receiving mail they don't want to get, mail that reduces their profits, their systems are chaotic. When it comes to billing you, their systems are never chaotic. And I mean: retaining my genetic material without my consent? It's insanely wrong. So—do you ever do this?—I tell her I'm an attorney and that I've got a bunch of hungry young associates who'll be all over this shakedown like a pack of wolves."

Ed says, "That would blow up in your face in Canada. We're—"

"In the U.S. it's different. In the U.S., you don't register on their systems unless you threaten a lawsuit. That's how they operate. Human reasonableness is just seen as an opening to make more money. So I said to Chris, Do you recall us ever getting a letter about a frozen sperm sample? She's like, I don't know, all those letters look the same. I'm like, Wait a minute, this is important, I want you to think hard. She's like, I can't do this, I've got to keep my eye on the ball. I'm like, What ball? This is the ball. I mean, think about it. My genes are in the hands of strangers. Never mind the nine hundred bucks. We're talking about my seed. For all I know, I could have children out there in the world right now. Offspring. It's far from impossible, right? Mistakes happen all the time. And foul play. People think that foul play doesn't really exist. They're wrong. Foul play is a very real thing, especially when there's money to be made. Believe me, I know."

Nobody has made a start on the cake or the assorted berries. I say to Jack Bail, "You're right to be concerned. You have to take care of this."

"That's what I did, Doc. Cut a long story short, I caved on the nine hundred bucks and I went to the clinic personally with the documentation. I made sure to get a receipt."

"That was smart," Chris says.

Jack Bail says, "I had no option: I got a letter from a debt collection agency. I had to cave. What was I going to do, risk my credit over nine hundred bucks? No, I had to cave. And I don't even know if they've actually disposed of the semen. I've got to assume they have. But I'll never know for sure, will I?"

Jack Bail spends the night on our sofa. In the morning, when Chris and I go down, there is a thank-you note.

Then a year passes and with it a tax season, and we

are walking on the beach, and I stop and I say to Chris, "You know what? We haven't heard from Jack Bail."

Our beach is a sand and shingle beach. The sand is a common blend of quartz and feldspar. The sand emerges from the ocean, so to speak, and continues inland until quite suddenly shingle replaces it. The shingle, or gravel, consists at first of pebbles, next of a mixture of pebbles and cobbles, and finally almost only of cobbles. This progressive distribution of the beach stones, apparently methodical, is in fact natural: a storm's waves will force rocks small and large landward, but retreating waves have less power and will move only smaller rocks seaward. The result is a graduated stranding of the rocks, which amass in a succession of steep slopes and berms. Our beach walk begins by scrambling down one berm and then a second, and I always take care to hold Chris's hand as we go down. Countless large spiders somehow make a life among the cobbles, and my job is to help Chris to put them out of her mind. Out of my mind, too. There are no leg-bugs out here. Leg-bugs are deer ticks. Every evening from May through November, Chris and I must examine each other for ticks. Sometimes we find one.

From the sand beach, the brown drumlin cliffs are exposed to our contemplation. The drumlins have been here since the Wisconsin glaciation. Their crosscut formation is the result of erosion by the ocean and the wind and the rain, a battering that is ongoing, I can testify after two winters here. As the hills retreat, they leave behind rock fragments that will, in due course, form part of the beach. This sort of fact is difficult for me to really understand; it must be said that much of my newly acquired geological knowledge is basically vocabularistic. I can't recognize feldspar, for example, or a granitic boulder. The Wisconsin glaciation isn't something I'm really on top of.

Chris and I scan the water, instinctively, I suppose. Sometimes we'll see a seal's head. It disappears for a while, then surfaces once more. They have large, cheerful, dog-like heads, these seals. It would feel good to see our warm-blooded kin out there today: this is one of those strolls when the up-close ocean daunts me more than a little, and as we skirt dainty rushes of water, I sense myself situated at the edge of an infinite and relentless eraser. I'm not sure that there's much to be done about this: awe, dread, wonder, and feelings of asymmetry come with the terrain. There must be something appealing about it, or we'd be elsewhere. Where, though? It's places that are going places. This part of Nova Scotia, the paleogeographers tell us, was once attached to Morocco.

"I hope he's OK," I say to Chris.

"I imagine he is," she says. She says, "You could always call him."

Yes, I could call him. But where would it end? I have taught, I once calculated, almost two thousand children.

No seal today. We keep walking. Chris says, "*The Last Fez.*"

I say, "About the Constantinople mission? We were sworn to silence about that."

Chris says, "Remember that night we crossed the Bosporus? With that surly boatman?"

"Ali the boatman?" I say. "How could I forget?"

The World of Cheese

◇

It had never occurred to Breda Morrissey that things might go seriously wrong between herself and her son, Patrick. But back in the fall he had declared her "persona non grata"—his actual expression—and pronounced that she was no longer permitted to have contact with her grandson, Joshua, on the grounds that she would be "an evil influence." It was a crazy, almost unbelievable turn of events, and all about such a strange matter—a scrap of skin.

Patrick disputed this. "This is not about *skin,* Mom," he said during the first session of the mother-son therapy they jointly underwent in New York. "Can't you see? That's not what this is *about.*"

Breda turned to the therapist, Dr. Goldstein—Dan, her son called him—for help. But Dr. Goldstein, whose dramatic beard and small pointy nose gave him, Breda thought, the look of a TV judge, was regarding her so severely that Breda was silenced.

Breda's reliving of this moment, as she sat in a window seat on the flight back to California, was interrupted by a nudge—a barge, almost—from her neighbor. This person was an obese woman of Breda's own age, mid-fifties, who from moment one had been tangling and fidgeting with carry-on luggage and safety instruction documents and in-flight entertainment gadgets. "Sorry," the woman breathed, continuing her struggle with the wires of her earphones. At the woman's other elbow, in the aisle seat, sat a littler person in a red sweater, a man. When drinks were served, the fat woman, as Breda thought of her, wordlessly helped herself to the little man's mini-pretzels packet. Breda understood with revulsion that they were a couple.

She looked out the window. An immense cloud floor covered the bottom of the void. Brilliant stacks of white vapor rose here and there, and pink haze lay beneath the blue upper atmosphere. It was a glorious, other-worldly spectacle of the kind that Breda, when she was a girl, would have found suggestive of winged horses and unknown realms; but what it came down to, when you grew up and looked through it all, Breda thought, was rain, rain falling on the fields and the forests and the houses and the people.

Breda kept gazing out. Something about the bumpy spread of cloud reminded her of cottage cheese, which in turn reminded her: Patrick had developed an interest in, as he put it, the world of cheese. During her stay, her son had each evening approached the dinner table with a cheeseboard, making bugling and fanfare noises. "Try this one, Mom," he said, pointing to one of the half-eaten, slightly stinking varieties, and Breda, who wondered whether these foodstuffs were legal, took a mouthful. "Nice," she said, refraining from any other comment—for example, that Patrick was obviously gain-ing weight as a result of his new hobby—for fear of provoking another outburst on his part. (And of course his wife, Judith, would no doubt be touchy, too. Everybody was touchy these days.) One night, Patrick announced that he and Judith and baby Joshua were taking a cheesing trip to Ireland. The plan was to go to the Kinsale International Gourmet Festival and then to drive from farmhouse to farmhouse, tasting semisoft rind-washed cheeses. "I'm not interested in hard cheeses," her son said importantly. If they found the time, he said, they'd drive up to County Limerick and maybe look up whoever was left of the ancestral Morrissey family.

"That'll be nice," Breda said.

In the early seventies, she and Patrick's father, Tommy, had taken the kids to a wonderful-sounding but actually dour looking village near the Shannon River, and had met remote Morrissey cousins of his, amorphous types who led unimaginable existences in cheap modern homes at the edge of the village and were nonplussed by their visitors. As she looked down at the clouds, Breda recalled two big things about that trip: it had rained the whole time, and everywhere they ran into people named Ryan. "It's raining Ryans," Tommy joked. "It's Ryaning hard."

Tommy, who a week after Patrick's wedding quit his biotech job and ran away to Costa Rica with the German woman. Packing his bags, he was the wronged furious one. "You make me feel like I'm vermin," he said, scrunching into his suitcase underpants Breda had just ironed. "With Ute I can bring up anything, absolutely anything. I can *be* anything. Jesus, I never knew what it was to feel alive. To think I've wasted all these years being made to feel a jerk, a creep. You want to know what we talked about last night? We talked about cunts

I have known. *Cunts I have known.* How they smell differently, how they're shaped differently, how they behave differently. Including your cunt. Oh yes. Do you know how special that is? Do you realize the level of trust and intimacy that takes?" On and on he went, appalling her. He began to shout. "Remember when I was alone in the Ukraine? All alone in that goddamn hotel and I get on the phone to my wife, my fucking *wife,* my one and only partner till death do us fucking part, and I asked you to say something for me, something with feeling, something that might connect us, anything at all. I'm not telling you to scrub floors or stick your hand in a pile of shit. I'm not ordering you to do anything. I'm *asking.* I'm *begging* for a sentence or two, that's all, just a few words, words a husband is entitled to expect from his wife. What do I get? Nothing! 'You know I don't do that kind of thing, Tommy.' *That kind of thing*? I'm howling for a drink in the fucking desert and you give me that shit? Well, fuck you, you uptight daddy's girl."

Breda was reexperiencing this horrifying episode because something about her son's recent harangues had put her in mind of his father.

As for the daddy's girl taunt, that went back forty years, to 1967, the year Breda traveled to Notre Dame for Tommy's graduation. Notre Dame was so Catholic and male that people on campus mistook her for a nun. After the ceremony, she and Tommy—they'd met six months before, at a wedding in Newport—set off on a cross-country drive to San Francisco. The plan was to return east in the fall so that Breda herself could start college. She started to feel sick just west of the Indiana border.

At first she thought it was the weed they'd been smoking, or maybe carsickness, but by the time they reached Missouri she knew she was pregnant. To celebrate, she and Tommy drove on to Reno and got married. When Breda rang home, her father answered the phone. He was a Boston lawyer. He found the whole thing—the trip to California, the jokey shotgun wedding, the long-distance pay phone shenanigans, the premarital sex—shocking. "Goddamn punk bullshit," he said, and hung up with a sob. When Breda tearfully redialed, her mother answered. "You'll have to forgive your father, sweetheart," she said. "It's just that these things have consequences. Maybe that's something you can't really understand at your age."

Breda patched things up with her parents, who came to see that she had married Tommy out of a sense of responsibility and not out of romantic whimsy. "It's a wonderful thing," Dad said when she became a mother. "And you're a wonderful girl."

Siobhan was born in the spring of 1968. Patrick came along two years later, named by Tommy for his father even though, to hear Tommy tell it, Grandpa Pat had barely acknowledged his own son. "He'd treat you like you'd treat a dog: ruffle your hair, take you for a walk in Van Cortlandt Park." This conversation took place one night soon after her father-in-law's death in 1975, when Tommy and she lay in the darkness of their Santa Barbara bedroom. "The best thing about Dad was he was a terrific whistler," Tommy whispered. "Oh, Jesus, he could whistle. He'd stick a thumb or pinkie in his mouth and shoot out this real earsplitter. He stopped taxis like they do in the movies." Tommy, shifting on his side, said, "You ever hear me whistle?"

"I think so," Breda said. "Sure."

"He taught me," Tommy said in a low voice. "He taught me how, Breda." His shoulder started to tremble, and Breda touched it.

Grandpa Pat was a New Yorker and passed his last years in a Midtown residential hotel. After his death they found his room filled with pepper shakers and salt shakers taken from the diners and bars in which he'd whiled away his days. Tommy displayed the shakers on a shelf at home. "Some families inherit sterling silver, others stolen restaurant utensils," he said. Later he asked Breda to box away the shakers because they made him think of the sands of time and depressed the hell out of him.

After Tommy disappeared to Costa Rica, Breda stayed put in the matrimonial home in Santa Barbara, unclear about where things stood. When it became apparent that her husband wasn't returning, she sold up and moved into an apartment in Atherton to be near Siobhan. Siobhan had urged the move. But within a year, Siobhan and her family headed east to Alexandria, Virginia. "Well, that's how it goes, I guess," Breda said when her daughter broke the news. "If you have to go, you have to go." Breda stayed in Atherton, working as an administrator for a medical practice. She took a weekly (and straightforward and pleasant) call from her son, and a biweekly (and difficult and tetchy) call from her daughter. Inevitably the latter put her through to the grandchildren. She called their names down the line and listened for a response. "Talk to Grandma," an adult instructed in the background. Then a child's voice, small and stubborn and distinct: "Don't want to."

From time to time, her children brought back news from the Switzerland of Central America, as Costa Rica was apparently known. It was so humid down there, Breda learned, that a paperback would practically rot overnight. It was also amazing. There were monkeys and colored birds and sloths and waterfalls and rocky beaches. Tommy, who had never been interested in the Californian ocean, allegedly took up surfing. There was a story that he'd saved a woman from being drowned, which Breda found hard to believe. More plausibly, he became a nature guide. He led groups into the forest and pointed out birds and termite hills. He had one trick, Patrick said, where he swung his machete into the bark of a tree, and sap—was it rubber?—came oozing out. When the hike was over, he took the surfers and eco-tourists and movie stars (apparently Tommy had rubbed shoulders with Woody Harrelson) for a bite to eat at the Crazy Toucan, which was the restaurant owned by the German woman. Patrick showed his mother snapshots of a wooden house with colored lights strung across the front porch. "See? That's where the bar is, right there. That outbuilding, that's the kitchen." "Nice," Breda said. "And there's Ute, with the blonde hair. She's a great cook. Fusion food." He pronounced the woman's name Ootah, as if he were an expert on Germany.

"Fusion food," Breda said. "Sounds good."

Breda and Tommy did not divorce. For a time, Breda was unsure which was worse: the mortification of divorce or the mortification of being so forgotten about that one's husband could not even bother to place one's breakup on a proper legal footing. Then Breda came to think, What difference does it really make, in the end? This question, she discovered, was increasingly applicable to a lot of things. It was true, as her mother had once remarked, that the consequentiality of things became clearer as you grew older, so that actions and especially omissions assumed an importance they never used to have; and so one grew more hesitant. But on the other hand it seemed to matter so much less whether you wound up with outcome A or outcome B.

Four years into their marriage, Patrick and Judith bought a house in the Bronx, not far from where Tommy had grown up. They held a housewarming party and Patrick made a big deal of it, insisting Breda fly over. "Bring your boyfriend, Mom," he joked. His father also turned up, with the German woman. When Breda offered to help out with the refreshments, Patrick said, "Just relax, Mom. Enjoy yourself. Leave the cooking to Ute. It's what she does for a living."

For an hour Breda mingled with the young people and played an agonizing game of hide-and-seek with the Costa Ricans. But a conversation with Tommy was inevitable. Emerging from the kitchen, he said jovially, "Hello, Breda." It was their first conversation since their separation, which also was four years old. He looked quite different. There was a beard and a ponytail, and his hands were cracked and brown. He was heavier, in spite of the surfing and the fusion food. "Good of you to come, Breda," he said, making her feel like an interloper. They made small talk. Breda noticed that Tommy made repeated use of a new expression. "The roads are kinda funky down there," he said of Costa Rica; and, "It's kinda funky meeting up again like this, isn't it?" No doubt this was beach talk or bar talk or surf talk. He had lost that exact, scientific air she'd once found attractive. A memory suddenly seized her: Tommy's liking for sniffing and snouting her ass while she took up a position on all fours; even, once, when she was menstruating and blood trickled down her inner thigh. "It's passion, honey," he mumbled. "This is passion."

As Breda ate parts of her in-flight meal, her thoughts circled again around the business with the foreskin.

It started when Judith learned from the ob-gyn that she was carrying a boy. Judith being Jewish, this raised the question of circumcision. Patrick was very against it. For two months it was all he wanted to talk to his mother about. "I'm saying *he* can circumcise himself," he said. "Let him grow up and let *him* decide."

"I guess," Breda said. She had her own preference, of course, but she didn't want to get involved.

"You guess?"

"No, no. You're right," Breda said.

Too late. He was off again, yelling. This business had turned him into a yeller. Sometimes she had to move the phone away from her ear. "There's no *guessing* here. It's either a yes or a no. Can he or can he not decide to become a Jew when he's older? *Yes.* Can he or can he not at that point have a circumcision if that's what he wants? *Yes.* If he grows up and decides to be a Christian, can he get his foreskin back? *No.* Case closed. End of discussion. But apparently not. You know what? I'm going to the doctor right now and I'm going to get it done on myself. I'm going to *demonstrate* it can be done, and then I'm not going to hear one more fucking word about it."

When Patrick came to the phone in a calmer mood, he was able to state Judith's case. "She's saying, what is he, a Jew or a pagan?" Maybe this is something they should have thought about earlier, Breda thought. "I'm saying, leave the kid alone. Then she says, It's more complicated. You have to carve out a Jewish space. There isn't any Jewish space out there. You have to carve it out."

Really? Breda felt like asking. In New York?

"I see," she said.

"Then there's her dad, of course. She says she doesn't know how he'd take it."

The dad, Harry, had spent three years as a little boy in a camp for Jews in Romania. But did he actually count as a Holocaust survivor? Breda wasn't a hundred percent sure. Unless she was mistaken, nobody in that camp got gassed or anything. It wasn't Auschwitz. But you could understand why he might take this issue seriously. And it made some of her son's arguments look a little lightweight, especially the ones having to do with penises. "Circumcision means loss of sensitivity," Patrick said. He'd looked it up on the Internet. He also said, "My son's dick should look like my dick. It's a father and son thing." Breda's judgment was that, come what may, Harry would live. Parents are a pretty sure bet.

She tried to inform herself. Her best friend in Atherton, Staccy Levingstone, who was Jewish, explained vaguely that cutting off the foreskin was all about removing a barrier to God—"impediment" was the word she used. Another friend, a Christian, told her that sometimes the mohel—the fellow who carried out the operation—cut the membrane beneath the foreskin using a long, sharp fingernail grown especially. Breda did not know what to make of this. Then Dr. Kentridge, one of the doctors at the practice where she worked, told her that Jewish circumcision was really a form of ritual bloodletting: Jewish law, he said, provided that a Jewish boy born without a foreskin must nevertheless have a drop of blood drawn from his penis. "Blood sacrifice, Breda," he said ominously, as if this should mean something to her.

Then everything suddenly turned upside down. Patrick saw it from Judith's point of view. His son would be named Joshua and would be a Jew. He could always convert to Christianity if he didn't like it. There would be a bris.

This was where Breda got into trouble. She e-mailed Patrick and Judith that she wouldn't be able to make it over for the bris. She gave no reasons.

Patrick replied:

I WILL NEVER FORGIVE YOU FOR THIS.

Terrified, Breda telephoned her son on three consecutive days. Each time he hung up. On the fourth day he consented to speak to her. "What?"

"I'm so sorry, my love," Breda said, in tears. "I've bought a ticket. I'm going to be there."

"We don't want you here. You're not welcome. Judith agrees."

"But why, honey? I've said sorry. I want to be there. I didn't know it meant so much to you."

"Are you out of your mind? Do have any idea what's going on here?"

Breda said, "Don't bully me, Patrick. Please."

"Bully? Is that it? You're calling me a bully?" The line went dead.

Breda rang her daughter. Siobhan, to whom impatience and certainty came easily, said, "Mom, it's totally his fault. He's just acting up."

"You really think so?" Breda gladly asked.

"Of course," Siobhan said. Breda heard a child

screaming in the background. "Can't you see what's going on here? He still hasn't grown up. He's still the baby of the family. He still has these infantile expectations about your responsibilities and your power. He has to have this big dramatic relationship with his mother. That's what you get if you treat him like a baby."

Breda was familiar with the complaint: how unfairly arduous Siobhan's life had been by comparison with her younger brother's, how Patrick always contrived to take the benefit of freebies—loans, airplane tickets, gifts—denied to Siobhan, how Patrick was the apple of her eye. "I guess," Breda said.

"I hate to say it, Mom, but you reap what you sow. Clark, stop it!" The boy kept on bawling. "Look, I've got to go," Siobhan said, and she hung up.

When Breda phoned Tommy in Costa Rica, he said, "I spoke to the kid already. He seemed kinda devastated, to be honest with you. You know, being here, surrounded by all these forests and wild places, it teaches you something. You learn to value the spiritual world." What junk! Breda silently shouted. You fraud! You and that fraud slut! "I kinda see why Patrick might have gotten worked up. The Jewish thing, Harry, the bris, Judith . . . You got to admit," Tommy said, "it's kinda funky."

Breda was upset. She, not Tommy, had always been the one Patrick spoke to when he needed to talk something over. And why hadn't Tommy gotten into trouble when he'd said he couldn't go to the bris because Ute would be in Germany and he had to look after the restaurant? Were employees nonexistent in Costa Rica?

She rang her son again. He said, "I'm not changing my mind. I want you to admit what's going on here."

Amazed by his vengefulness, she said, "This is a very

emotional thing. You're very upset. I understand completely."

"Yeah, right," Patrick said.

"Patrick, please, it was an honest mistake."

"Yeah, like the Holocaust was an honest mistake."

"I don't understand," Breda said. She felt ill. She had no idea how to extricate herself from this. "What am I supposed to be admitting? What have I done that's so wrong?"

Patrick became excited. "It's what you *didn't* do. You never took this thing seriously. You kept your distance. You stood by. I know why now. It's super-clear. You never liked it when I married Judith and you can't accept that Joshua is being brought up as a Jew. You resent it. That's what this is all about. Anti-Semitism. It killed six million people. It would have killed my own son. I can't live with that."

And so, using the phrase "persona non grata," he banned her from having dealings with his family. After the bris, it took Tommy's far-off intervention to set up an encounter at the office of Dr. Goldstein, in New York. (At Breda's expense. Patrick said, "I really, really don't see myself picking up the tab here.")

Patrick repeated his accusation of anti-Semitism in the second of the three sessions they had with Dr. Goldstein. Breda denied it but, seeing that Dr. Goldstein and Patrick were not going to let the matter drop, and dreading any prolongation of the discussion, she quickly stated that maybe at some level she was opposed to Patrick's marriage to a Jewish woman and that maybe she had found the whole business with the foreskin distasteful and that maybe this did have something to do with what had happened. Dr. Goldstein said, "Well done, Breda. That must have been hard for you." He explained, "Because of the Holocaust and slavery and everything we now know about prejudice, there's a kind of taboo about acknowledging group preferences. But actually everybody is naturally biased in favor of their own kind and their own traditions." A further session and a half were devoted to this subject and to Patrick's "feelings of disappointment." (God, how sensitive men were—on the subject of themselves.) Undertakings of mutual compassion were exchanged, and Dr. Goldstein privately suggested to Breda that "a gesture of reparation" might be a good idea. And that, it appeared, was that. The crisis was over. Speaking for himself, Patrick said, he would forgive and forget. "But, Mom, I'll just say one last thing: one day, your grandson will know that you never came to his bris. That's something you'll always have to live with."

Well, Breda said to herself on the plane, if Joshua at some point in the future cared to think about the episode at all, he would no doubt understand that she was not in any way to blame.

It was around ten PM California time, and dark outside. Ordinarily they would have been landing right about now, but their departure from New York had been delayed by thunderstorms. Breda closed her eyes. She was on the point of falling asleep when the fat woman, reaching for an overhead button, jolted her. "Excuse me," the woman called loudly to a flight attendant. "Excuse me."

"Myra, stop it," her husband hissed.

"Well, I'm not like you. You'd wait years."

"You have to learn to be patient. And I wouldn't wait years. That's an exaggeration."

Breda opened her eyes and closed them again. Now her neighbors were talking about the wife's recent visit to a doctor.

"I'm so fat," the wife said, "they couldn't draw my blood."

"Sometimes they have problems finding a vein in a person with more flesh on their arm," the husband said.

"I feel like I don't have any blood," the woman wailed.

"Myra, that's stupid," the husband said.

"I didn't know I didn't have a vein there."

"It's not that you don't have a vein. It's that they can't find it. Come on, baby, you know that."

"Yes, well, I don't like it."

Wholly sleepless, Breda thought about the question of reparation. She didn't like the word one bit. It made her sound like a war criminal. But an idea nonetheless came to her: why not commission a special wooden bench for her son and grandson? They could sit on it, talk, whatever. It could be their spot. A bench would be easy to maintain. They could place it in the garden or, better still, in a public space—like Van Cortlandt Park, where Tommy and Grandpa Pat had walked together. The bench would have an inscription, of course, recording a grandmother's gift. That way three, maybe even four generations would be united. The idea came to Breda from what she'd seen in London, where the parks and squares seemed to be filled with benches donated by Americans who had fallen in love with that city. The benches evoked long-gone people and times—the war years, so often—but in their beautiful English setting they seemed indestructibly romantic. Breda, whose one trip to London had taken place in the aftermath of her father's death, had considered dedicating such a bench over there to his memory, but she eventually decided that it wouldn't make much sense since Dad had only been to London for two business trips and had no real ties to the place—Dad, who now lay with Mom in a treeless Boston graveyard.

But to where, or to what, do we have ties? Breda wondered. The world seemed more dreamlike by the day. Mornings were fine: waking up, driving to work, applying herself to her work, eating lunch. But then, sallying on through the afternoon and into the evenings, she would find herself doubting the solidity of everything around her. Each moment, it seemed, was barely distinguishable from some past or even prospective moment. And during her visit to New York, she had been persistently attacked by a sense that the family scenes taking place around her, each an intense variation on some previous scene, were no more or less substantial than a TV rerun. She found herself depressed by Joshua's musical plastic turtle, which, its batteries dying, emitted a slow and gasping and terrible rendition of "Row, Row, Row Your Boat." When her son and grandson and daughter-in-law kissed her goodbye at the airport, she heard herself blurt out, "You're here now, and yet in a minute you'll all be gone."

Breda, eyes closed, found herself thinking of a childhood friend, Cynthia Byrne, who not long ago had gone back to college to take a Biblical Studies course. Cynthia had been a churchgoing Catholic all her life, and Breda was a little shocked to hear her announce, a year into her studies, that the Bible was a relatively youthful, and certainly plagiaristic, set of myths. Breda could not remember the details of Cynthia's statements, but it came down to this: much of the Old Testament was derived from preexisting Syrian or Assyrian or Babylonian sources. The Jews never fled from Egypt and had always lived in Israel. Moses was as make-believe as Mickey Mouse. King David, too, probably. The great stories of the Old Testament had been dreamt up in order to boost certain Jewish tribes at the expense of other Jewish tribes. "Like so much history," Cynthia told her, "those myths were essentially an exercise in self-glorification and self-legitimization. Beautiful, yes; powerful, yes; but factually bunk." "Well, if you say so," Breda said. "*I'm not saying anything*," Cynthia said sharply. "This is standard scholarship. Ask anybody who knows anything about it."

Although Breda's capacity for belief in God had long since abandoned her, she was troubled by Cynthia's dismissal of the ancient faiths. Then again, she had always felt that there was something fishy about Judaism, a religion that, unless she was mistaken, offered little or no prospect of life after death. The Jews were supposed to twist up their lives with prayers and wig-wearing and food rules—for what? Christianity and Islam were strange, too, but at least they promised heaven. Of course, any confidence in heaven began to crumble once you gave it thought; but then everything crumbled once you thought about it, everything you'd been led to believe was true and transcendent.

Her eyes were now open. She felt the plane thudding down through clouds, then saw earthly lights, patterned and hopeful. She felt ashamed. Her son wanted a world with a further dimension for him and his family. She made it difficult for them. She dragged them down.

The plane landed in Oakland at one o'clock in the morning, three hours behind schedule. There followed an infuriating delay with the baggage, and it was not until three that Breda was finally able to push her cart toward the taxi stand. But there were no taxis, and the line seemed miles long. As Breda stood despairingly by the curb, a black man walked by muttering, "Taxi, taxi," and Breda tried to summon the courage to take up his offer, even though he was illegal-looking. Then another traveler, a businessman, appeared from behind her and decisively signaled to the black man. "Park Plaza Hotel," the businessman said.

The taxi driver waved his hand. "No, no, I not driving for just one mile."

The businessman had anticipated this answer and waved a twenty-dollar bill. This struck Breda as an act of awesome worldliness.

The driver hesitated, then said, "OK," and walked off to collect his car.

It occurred to Breda that she was a few minutes away from a clean hotel bed, whereas it might be two exhausting hours before she arrived home. She looked again at the businessman. She opened her mouth for a second or two, then finally spoke. "Excuse me," she said, "but did I hear you say you're going to a hotel?"

The man turned to her. He was pale-haired, sturdily built, mid-forties. "I guess I am." He paused. "You, ah, need a ride?"

The accent was southern. "Well, I was thinking," Breda said, "it doesn't look like there's much sense in waiting here."

"I'd be happy to take you," he said, looking neither happy nor unhappy.

"Thank you," Breda said.

They stood awkwardly together until the car arrived. The businessman helped Breda with her luggage. There was something appealing about him, Breda thought—something about the athletic swing he gave her suitcase, something about his purposeful air. Breda got into the backseat and waited while the businessman placed his own things into the trunk. Then he eased down next to Breda and slammed shut the passenger door with a slight bodily lurch. His shoulder made contact with hers, and Breda experienced a shock of sexual arousal of a kind she had no live memory of.

The hotel was almost comically close by, and they arrived after what seemed like a few seconds' drive. When Breda offered the man money, he said, "No, really, there's no need," and quickly got out of the car. He picked up his bags and walked immediately to the hotel, leaving Breda to handle her own suitcase.

Breda took no offense. When she entered the hotel lobby, the businessman was talking to the woman at the check-in desk. Breda got in line behind him.

"Marietta, Georgia," the woman was saying as she typed the man's address into her computer.

"That's right," the man said.

The woman typed on. "Guess you pronounce it Muh-retta, huh?"

"I might."

She tittered. She was a blonde, in her forties. "My

brother lived right there, in Marietta. Now he lives—you'd never guess where."

"I give up," the man said. Breda couldn't tell from his voice whether he was enjoying himself or not. She moved to one side to get a view of his face.

"Siberia," the receptionist said. "Bought some land there with his Russian girlfriend." She handed him a card-key for his room. Room 207, Breda had already noted.

"He bought a property in Siberia?" The man was now alert. "He can get his title insured over there?"

"I don't know. I guess."

"If I can't insure my title," the man said, "if I can't get copper-bottomed title insurance, I don't touch it."

Breda found the man's strong opinion on title insurance impressive. She watched him as he walked over to the elevator.

She was given room 214, which was, it turned out, only two doors across the corridor from room 207. It was almost four o'clock, but Breda took a shower. Afterward, she examined her body in the bathroom mirror. Her face she had never liked—she saw a thin upper lip, hair that had never, not even for ten minutes, been cut or styled right—but she could quite neutrally say that her body had not really changed in a couple of decades. Not significantly. As she fastened the towel around her chest, Breda wondered, and allowed herself to doubt, if the businessman's wife could claim as much. That was assuming he had a wife, which was uncertain, since he hadn't worn a wedding band. Breda decided to proceed on the footing that he was unmarried, or at least unattached.

She caught herself. Proceed? Proceed where? And how, and to what end? She closed her eyes with embarrassment. He had shown no sign of being attracted to her, was at least five years younger, and by now was almost certainly asleep. What was she thinking of doing? Tiptoeing out into the hallway and knocking on his door? It was crazy, out of the question; but it seemed also out of the question to not do anything. Not to be with this man seemed a grotesque impossibility, like the impossibility of perpetual death.

Breda splashed cold water on her face. What was happening to her? She had lost all sense of the real and the unreal. Wake up! she urged her reflection. But here was a reality: the man was only thirty feet away. Thirty feet! And if she went out and stood by his door, it would only be twelve feet! And if she knocked on his door, well the worst that could happen would be a rejection; whereas the upside . . . Breda unfastened the towel and let it fall to the floor. Still looking into the mirror, she arched her back and stuck out her ass. White, like a cloud, she thought. She wished it were rounder, though. She wished . . . She shut her eyes. Enough.

But once back in the bedroom, she found herself fumbling into a bra and panties. They were new from Garnet Hill and though perhaps not sexy, then certainly pretty. What to wear with them, though? Her nightgown, with its faded floral, was out of the question, and there was no hotel bathrobe. Breda picked up her raincoat. A raincoat over underwear. It was a combination that brought to mind Faye Dunaway. Faye Dunaway—the most stylish woman in the world, in Breda's eyes, at least before all that plastic surgery—would walk right over to room 207, knock on the door, and, with a bra cup showing beneath her mackintosh, ask for a light.

The raincoat felt cold against her skin. It laid bare

her neck and the pleated skin near her collarbone. Breda turned up the collar, tightened the belt, and examined herself again. She left the bathroom.

She lay down on the bed in her raincoat. She was suddenly exhausted and, in that increasingly familiar and frightening way, adrift—from the world of Faye Dunaway, of children, of cheese. She would be buried with her father and mother in the Boston graveyard. It was with this thought that she found calmness and, still wearing her raincoat, sleep.

The Referees

◇

I'm having lunch with a friend from college days, Michael, with the secret purpose of asking him a favor. It's not the only reason I'm meeting him. I like Michael, as one does. He's entertaining. He decides to tell me about his neighbor, Gus—

"Gus?" I say. "Are we talking Augustus?"

"Gustavus," Michael says.

—who has, apparently, been ill-tempered and hostile for years—

"Back up," I say. "Gustavus? As in Gustavus Adolphus?"

"What? He's Gustavus Goldman. Gus Goldman."

—this guy, this Gus, who lives in the apartment next door to Michael's and has a history of irascibility and unhelpfulness connected, it would seem, to his alcoholism, this guy has turned over a new leaf and is now a sober, much happier, downright pleasant individual, and for some months has been trying to befriend my friend Michael, and has been Miking him—

"Did you say 'Miking' you?"

Michael says, "You know, 'Mike' this, 'Mike' that."

"Oh yeah, right."

—Miking him with a view to Michael becoming his pal. But Michael doesn't want to be pals with Gus. He doesn't like the guy, even if the guy who he doesn't like has been replaced by a much sunnier and more affable non-asshole who sort of merits being befriended and who no doubt would appreciate Michael's support and affirmation as he ventures down the straight and narrow—

"Hold on," I say. "How was he an asshole? What did he do, exactly?"

"Do? He was an asshole. He behaved like an asshole."

"You're saying he was unneighborly."

"I'm not saying that. I don't *need* to say that. I'm saying I'll be the judge of whether he's an asshole or not. That's my *prerogative*. It's not an objective test. It doesn't matter if nine out of ten people think he's terrific. It doesn't matter if he's the greatest neighbor of all time. I get to decide who I'm going to be friends with, in accordance with my criteria."

"For sure," I say. "Freedom of association."

Michael, who is an attorney, says, "Well, that's a slightly different concept."

—anyhow, so Gus is on the wagon and offering Michael his friendship, and the question that must be answered, never losing sight of the fact that Michael enjoys a basically unqualified freedom to keep whomsoever at whatever distance he sees fit to keep them for whatever reason, the question to be answered is—

I say, "The answer is no. Don't do it. An asshole is an asshole. Don't cave."

—the question to be *answered*, Michael goes on, isn't

whether he should be Gus's friend, which is never going to happen, you can't just undo years and years of being a dick, life just doesn't work like that, no, the question is how to *manage* the situation so that *Michael* isn't suddenly the asshole; because, although being an asshole would be within Michael's rights—

"Correct. You get to be an asshole. It's not illegal."

—being an asshole isn't what he *wants;* and, as things stand, it's Gus who's the nice guy and it's Michael who's the asshole.

My friend is bark-laughing. It's a bark-laugh I remember well, and it's as if we're once again at NYU, in the dorm on Thirteenth Street. I say, "Yeah, that's right, someone has to be the asshole. And it can't be Gus. Not anymore. He's turned over a new leaf. Gus is nice now."

Michael says, "It's like the poker thing. If you look around the table and can't figure out who the asshole is—guess what? It's *you.*"

The old back-and-forth is still there, the old badinage, the old rapport; and with pleasure we finish our hamburgers and catch up on each other's news. Mine is the more interesting news, I would say, what with my interesting divorce and my interesting pennilessness and my interesting loneliness on my recent return to New York from Portland, Oregon, but Michael has anecdotes that he wants to share, and I end up not saying very much, and it's only at the last minute that I'm able to mention that I'm trying to rent an apartment in Prospect Heights. "It's a co-op," I tell him. "They need me to provide character references. Hey, Mike," I say with the old merrymaking irony, "could you write me one? You've got stationery. They'll like that."

We're splitting the check: Michael puts the full amount on a law-firm credit card and I pay him my half in cash. "Sure," he says. We shake hands. "E-mail me."

Which is, when I get back to the office, exactly what I do. Michael replies within the hour:

> Hi, Rob. On reflection, I don't think I can do this. I've consulted some people here, and they agree that, as a professional matter, a historic collegiate acquaintance is an inadequate basis for a personal reference. It would be a different story if I had firsthand knowledge of your life post-college. I thought it right to let you know as promptly as possible. Michael.

What an asshole, I think I can say.

It wouldn't matter except for the fact that it does matter. I need two character references ASAP, and so far I've failed to collect a single one.

That's not totally accurate. I've got this, from Tariq:

> To Whom It May Concern: As his work supervisor, I have known Rob Karlsson for two weeks, during which time he has presented as a pleasant and responsible person. I hope this is of assistance.

Tariq is British and so maybe is guided by some protocol of understatement that I'm not familiar with. Either way, his endorsement, as worded, isn't what I'm looking for. I'm informed by the apartment lessor, Travis, who's twenty-six and some kind of junior restaurant manager and yet somehow also a man of property, that the co-operators require (per their forwarded e-mail) "meaningful letters of reference that specifically address the high standards of integrity and deportment expected of a co-operative resident."

I get that it's a little much to drop this thing on Tariq, but in the short time we've known each other we've worked well together on our project, and I'd like to think that we've made a social connection that's not unreal over the course of our almost nightly after-work drinks, when he goes from being my superior at the office to being just a dude who would like me to introduce him to a girl who would like to be introduced to him. I can't help him with this, unfortunately. After years on the West Coast, my New York contacts are pretty much vestigial. It took some effort to track down Paul, on whose couch I'm currently sleeping, if that's the right word for what an insomniac does, and I can't even claim that Paul, my mother's cousin's son, was anything like a huge bud in the first place, and in all honesty I tracked down Paul not because he was Paul as such but because the poor devil was the only New Yorker I knew who was likely to be kind enough to let me crash with him until I found somewhere more permanent and suitable. Paul himself essentially lives at his boyfriend's place, in Manhattan; since the key handover we've laid eyes on each other only once. I've of course asked him for a reference and, because he's a reliable and upstanding person who's known me (very slightly, admittedly) since we were kids and is technically family, I can count on him to come through, I think, even though his job keeps him very busy and more than a week has passed since he agreed to do the necessary and time is getting to be of the essence.

What I mustn't do is give the wrong kind of credence to the apparent fact that, at the age of thirty-six, I find myself unable to easily identify two people who know me well enough to plausibly and candidly state that I'm a sufficiently OK human being for the purpose of living in close vicinity to others. That would be a superficial and overly catastrophic way of looking at things.

Now this, just in, from Portland:

> Robert, I'm glad to hear you have found an apartment you like. I've been worried about you. It's good to see that you're doing fine. I'm going to ask you not to contact me for a long while. It's unhealthy for us to be involved in each other's lives. That's why I'm not going to give you the personal recommendation you asked for. I'm sure you understand. Good luck with everything, Robert. Samantha.
>
> Have you asked Billy?

I want to write back to Samantha to make it clear that I'm not looking for any further involvement in her life but actually and merely asking for a onetime administrative courtesy. I also want to contest her bare assertion that I'm "doing fine," which I feel is basically a way to throw a blanket over me and my situation as if I were a small fire that you put out, and—wait: Billy?

Billy who?

Samantha doesn't e-mail back. But Travis texts:

Got those refs yet? Need to wrap this up.

Oh—*Billy*.

Billy is my childhood best friend. We haven't been in touch for nearly a decade. That's been my doing, I've got to say. Billy came to "NYC," as he always called it, in his mid-twenties, not long after he'd belatedly gathered the credits he needed for a business degree from Mankato State, and for a little more than a year he hung out with me and Samantha nonstop, it felt like, and kept hitting on Samantha's friends with no luck, often implicating me as his "wingman," and dragged me out to hockey games I absolutely didn't want to go to. Billy, at this time, worked in sales strategy for a baby food company, in Midtown. His dream was to come up with a world-conquering idea for a "startup," and he and I spent many evenings drinking beer at my place, when, if we weren't re-reminiscing about the characters and events of our teenage years in St. Paul, we were contemplating the magical "synergy" that Billy thought would be achieved by "fusing" his business skills and my computer expertise. Often, I remember, he would tap his skull with his finger and say that it, his skull, contained "the keys to the kingdom." Meanwhile, Samantha lay low in the bedroom. It was an unsustainable state of affairs. Billy is a lovely, somewhat special guy, no question, and not at all malicious, but his company became intolerably stressful. Also, he developed a habit of reprimanding me. For example, if I voiced a mildly negative thought—"This coffee is too weak," say, or "I wish those bros would turn down the volume"—Billy would say something like, "Dude, chill, you're getting all snobby in your old age," and say it with a weird laugh of anger. I kept wishing that my old friend would somehow change or wise up or move on, but if anything he doubled down on who he thought he was, with the result that a kind of cartoon Minnesotan Billy came into being, an extremist of easy-goingness who could be counted on to occupy the nice or feel-good side of any issue and make everyone else feel cynical and shitty by comparison. It took a drawn-out and horrible process of rejection by me of him to bring our relationship to an end. I really believe that the trauma surrounding that whole episode is why I was so enthusiastic about leaving the city, where I'd spent eight otherwise happy and productive years, in order to relocate to Portland, where Samantha had a job offer from Wieden+Kennedy and I'd lined up a sweet-looking gig to develop software for a real-life startup that had as its goal the revolutionizing of the logistics industry.

Though incommunicado, Billy and I have remained friended on Facebook. That's how I know he's still in the tristate area, working as a regional sales director, which sounds hopeful. As does the fact that he's married, with two daughters. But I really don't want to be in touch with him again, not unless it's some kind of emergency.

> Hey, Billy. All good? Looks like I'm back in NYC. Samantha and I have split. Long story. Not good. Can't talk about it without beers. Listen, can you do me a solid? I'm in a hole.

Then I type out my plea for a reference letter, and send it, and go to bed.

Travis I've texted:

> No worries. Stand by.

◇

This isn't totally disingenuous. I've sent messages to two trustworthy people in Portland: my old startup comrade Halil; and Courtney, who is first and foremost Samantha's friend but who I hit it off with independently, I feel. It's not ideal to have out-of-towners as my referees, since there may be a perception that they won't truly grasp the demanding norms that New York co-operators abide by, but whatever.

Cousin Paul, in response to my reminder, e-mails:

> Hi Rob so sorry about this could you write it for me?? Crazy busy . . . I'll sign off to whatever you write . . . THX . . .

In the morning, I see that Halil has still not replied. That's not what I expected. When the startup finally collapsed, which happened roughly at the same second that my marriage did, Halil was the guy who went in for farewell eye-locking, chest-bumping, and phrases like "blood brother" and "muchacho."

Courtney has gotten back to me:

> Rob, this is difficult for me to write.
>
> This past year I've been very close to Sam as she has gone through this difficult time. She has shared many things with me about what her experience has been. I have to say that I've found it painful on many levels. I feel bad that I wasn't able to see what was going on and that I wasn't there for her when she needed me. I owe her my focus now. So I'm going to have to recuse myself

from what you're asking for. This doesn't reflect
on you at all. This is just about me taking owner-
ship of what I need to do.

What does this e-mail even mean? She wants to recuse
herself? Who is she, Sonia Sotomayor?

I can only control the things I can control. Like writing Paul's letter. That's something I can take care of right
away.

But patting myself on the back, even with an alter
ego, is challenging. For support, I go online. There I find
plenty of helpful pro forma character references, even
though they're for people in situations different from
mine—i.e., people who are applying for jobs or intern-
ships or fellowships, not people seeking admission to a
residential building.

I've got to say, I'm a little taken aback. I accept that
I'm looking at invented documents and persons, but
we're in the realm of realism, surely, and the referrers,
even if concocted, are quite outstanding. Joe is stellar
and can-do and masterly and explains complex systems
very well. Mary has grit and gentleness, compassion and
superb forensic skills. Arturo is loyal, determined, and
reasonable. The most powerful commendations tell little
stories: how Emily showed terrific leadership during the
power outage; how Ken handled an ultra-demanding cli-
ent with the sensitivity and effectiveness that have come
to be expected of him. The letter in support of Annie,
written by her high school teacher, is actually moving
in its depiction of a young woman's industriousness and
precocious commitment to social justice. There are a lot
of ethical, pleasant, and dependable people notionally

out there. It's intimidating, frankly. I had no idea the bar
was so high.

When I get back from work, a tiny bit drunk after
a few shots with Tariq, there's a FedEx packet leaning
against the door, and I see that it's for me, and I rip the
thing open. It contains an envelope. My name appears
on the envelope, in Billy's graceful handwriting.

I get myself a beer and take a seat at Paul's kitchen
table.

Billy: when he came east, he stayed with Samantha
and me in Williamsburg until he found a room in Manhattan. Brooklyn was out of the question; he had to have
a Manhattan address. It was a question of dignity, I suppose, as was his insistence on having "wheels." He was
probably my only New York friend with a car. This came
to an end when he was involved in a small collision on
the FDR and had no option but to plead guilty to DWUI
(weed) and to accept a one-year revocation of his license.
I accompanied Billy to court, wearing a suit and tie in
solidarity. Afterward we lit up cigarettes on the steps of
the courthouse, even though I'd quit smoking. We had a
laugh at the expense of the prosecutor, an unfortunate-
looking guy who I'd spotted in the bathroom, mysteriously throwing up. Not much else was talked about.
It was a sunny day, and we sat next to each other in
our suits and shades, smoking and feeling good and, in
our minds, looking good. There was something totally
canned and anachronistic about the moment, of course,
but it was special nonetheless, and for me the highlight of
our friendship's I'd have to say tragic New York phase.

The envelope is high-quality ivory, as is the letter
paper, which has been folded into perfect thirds. Billy's

really gone the whole hog. It being an official document, I wash my hands before I open and read it:

FUCK. YOU. ASSHOLE.

OK—that's not nice. That is really quite hurtful.

Although, when I visualize Billy scheming and finessing all the details—the insult, the fancy notepaper, the same-day delivery—I have to smile.

> It is with great pleasure that I commend Robert Karlsson to you. Robert and I have cohabited in my small apartment for several months. In all candor, it has been an entirely harmonious and agreeable experience. Robert has at all times been quiet, helpful, considerate, tidy, and charming—everything one could hope for in a fellow resident. This comes as no surprise, since I have known Robert and his family for over twenty years. I vouch for him without hesitation or qualification. Any co-operative should feel fortunate to have him.
>
> Please feel free to contact me at any time to discuss this matter further.
>
> Yours truly, Paul Robson.

How easy was that? I'd even say it was enjoyable. And I don't think it's bullshit. Put it this way: I very much doubt that those whom it concerns will complain, down the road, that they were fundamentally misled, because what's fundamental is what I'm like, not whether some statement about me is a lie that's either white or off-white. I honestly believe that I'm someone who doesn't make trouble, certainly not for my neighbors. To Whom

It May Concern: Relax. Rob Karlsson will not make your life a misery. I have known him longer than just about anybody, and I should know. This is the guy who, as a fourteen-year-old Boy Scout, went on a two-day hiking trip in the Quetico wilderness with Simon Burch, and carried both his and Simon's rucksacks on the five-mile trek back to base camp after Simon hurt his back. This is the guy who wouldn't squeal on Wally Waters after Wally had pushed him down the stairs and the principal demanded to know exactly what had happened. This Rob Karlsson is the Bobby Karlsson who pretended he'd hurt his throwing arm so that Carlos Rodriguez could finally pitch an inning. This is whom we're concerned with here. With the first boy Amanda McAteer kissed, who never told anybody about it because Amanda didn't want it to get around. Who in college volunteered for Citymeals on Wheels (albeit unreliably and briefly). Who definitely has no criminal record. Who is something of a sinner and a screwup, definitely, but whose "heart is in the right place," according to a certain person with credibility on this issue. Who is co-operative by nature, as nobody can deny. Who refrains from unkindness when commenting online, even when drunk and using a pseudonym. Who was a good kid, his father once said. Who when little accompanied his father on rambles, and grew interested in wildflowers, learning about the common yarrow, the jack-in-the-pulpit, and the spoon-leaf sundew, which he remembers only because of their impressive names and not because they are still identifiable by him, which they're not. Who liked most of all to walk in the forest, in fact liked the word "forest," though not as much as the word "glade," and was always asking his father, Dad, is this a glade?

Promises, Promises

◇

In memory of David Foster Wallace

They'd promised an ocean view, and they'd delivered. Down below was indeed the ocean, with waves that again and again made little white tassels, as if what might actually be on view were a vast, vastly repetitive unfurling of blue and green rugs. It was six in the morning. Six surfers, sitting on their boards, had the water to themselves.

Fritz shouted out, "Coffee?" and Anne, twisting, shouted in, "No thanks."

She turned back in time to see the sextet spring up and go. Then she saw that farther out, much farther out, the water held a little black head. The swimmer was going directly away from the shore. Anne watched him—"him," because she perceived something masculine about the movement of the arms. He kept going out, out.

"How far would you say he is?" she asked Fritz.

Fritz took a slurp of coffee. "I'd say half a mile." If Fritz sounded expert, which he did, it was because back in Tucson they owned a lap pool in which every morning

Fritz swam seventy-two laps, which came to a mile, he reckoned, and Anne wasn't about to check his calculations. She never swam in the lap pool. She found the blue coffin of water oppressive, just as she found oppressive the gym next door to her downtown office, a tank of light in which a row of runners nightly ran toward the window.

They watched the swimmer. "Every beach has one," Fritz said. "It's compulsory under the Beach Dramatis Personae Act of 1972. There's the three hot chicks walking in the surf, there's the kid with the bucket, and there's the guy swimming out toward the horizon."

Anne, who had heard variations on this joke before, said nothing. Her attention was on the seafarer. He was completely on his own. Every stroke out was a stroke he'd have to take back, therefore every stroke counted double. But she wasn't counting.

The Death of Billy Joel

◇

For his fortieth birthday, Tom Rourke organizes a golf trip to Florida. He e-mails a total of ten men, but only three say yes. A few, including some of his oldest and, historically and theoretically, best friends, do not even summon the energy to reply. Two of the three who agree to join him, Aaron and Mick, are his regular golfing partners in New York and friends of only a few years' vintage. Only the final member of the quartet, David, was at college with Tom back in the eighties. David now lives in Chicago. Tom hasn't seen David in a long time, and hanging out with him is one of the things he's most looking forward to.

It would have surprised the Tom of twenty years ago, when he and his contemporaries clambered aboard the world with a piratical energy he now finds marvelous, to have learned that only one of his undergraduate shipmates would answer such an important summons. But the Tom of today is not surprised, or even disappointed. A foursome is perfect for a golf trip. And if he is to walk the plank into his forties—and it seems, a little incredibly, that he must—then Aaron and Mick and David, who are more or less his own age, will make fine witnesses. Tom is not too concerned about the milestone, at least not yet, because he has almost a month of his thirties left. The only moment of alarm comes when his mother, on the phone from Connecticut, says, "Let me tell you, the years between forty and fifty go by in a flash." The remark both scares and disappoints him: she has failed in her never-ending duty, thinks Tom, who not without guilt has created two children of his own, to make the business of life and death seem less frightening to him.

Tom makes all the arrangements. He books the hotel rooms and the tee times and three round-trip tickets to Tampa/St. Petersburg. (David is combining the Florida outing with a business trip to Nashville, and will make his own travel arrangements.) The New York–Tampa–New York tickets are only $230, taxes included, but that does not stop his companions from wondering out loud, in the taxi to LaGuardia, if Tom might not have gotten a cheaper deal. "I got them on Travelocity," Tom says. "They were the cheapest available." He is handing out the sheets of paper, printed out from the Web, that now pass for airplane tickets.

Aaron says, "You didn't try JetBlue? JetBlue doesn't turn up on Travelocity."

"Yeah, well, these are the tickets I got," Tom, a little vexed, says. Aaron knows more than he does about food, bars, music, anime, cocktails, clothes, and, Tom has now been reminded, the Internet. Of course, Aaron has the time to investigate such things, now that he's separated from his wife and son and spending much of his time with a brand-new twenty-six-year-old Venezuelan girlfriend.

The three New Yorkers fly off, separately seated in window seats. Each, it seems to Tom, is glad to be left alone to moon out of a thick plastic porthole undisturbed. Exactly what is being mulled over, Tom cannot say. The men's encounters are almost wholly confined to golf games, and the possibilities of self-revelation are few in the introspective cosmos of each round, in which the players, roving as couples in buzzing carts, deal mainly in tactful silences, terse or cheerful words of forgiveness and encouragement, and cackling monetary calculation. Tom presumes—not overly gloomily, he thinks— that his friends are grappling with the shaming inward puzzle that, in the last year or so, has come to preoccupy him: how the principal motions of his life—those involving his tolerant and industrious wife, his daughters, his decently affirmative work—have largely, and for reasons he cannot put his finger on, been reduced to a mere likeness of vitality. Which perhaps explains his and his friends' increasingly inordinate gratefulness for golf. Certainly, being out on the course is one of the few times Tom is convinced of his so-called place in the universe— convinced even though he understands that this adventure with golf, a cliché, expands the funnel of triteness through which his existence ever more rapidly pours.

Queens, when they fly over it, is all snow and inky roads, a newspaper made panoramic. The Hudson, Tom next sees, is mottled by large, semitransparent plaques of ice. It has been a freezing, miserable start to 2004, the second coldest January in half a century, and he feels an enormous relief to be migrating south. At Tampa, the plane swoops around a bay made exotic by spectacular swirls of turquoise. The men all crane to see out, for it's their first time in Tampa. The land down there looks watery and flat and generously quadrangular: the roofs, the lots, the blocks, the lagoons, all have a squarish spaciousness to them. It is a gloomy morning but not, according to the pilot, a cold one. Tom remembers how earlier in the month, when the temperature fell to one degree, the monstrous cold was uncannily invisible in the sunlit city; it agitates him, this recollection of the vicious unseen. Then he spots the ribbon-like fairways of a golf course, innocuous and pointless-looking from the plane, and is calmed.

At the airport, things go well. Their clubs and bags are practically the first to emerge on the carousel—Tom feels a lurch of emotion at the sight of his small brown leather overnight bag bravely holding its own among thuggish black cases—and they have no trouble finding the Hertz office. Although Tom has booked a midsize sedan, Aaron secures an upgrade to an SUV. They argue mildly on the drive to Clearwater about SUVs and their propensity to kill other road users and flip over, but underneath it all they are excited: to everybody's disbelief, none of them has ridden in an SUV before. The most pleasing feature of the vehicle is its satellite radio. Neither Tom nor Mick knows how to work it but Aaron, of course, does. He finds a rap channel—fucking this and motherfucker that, which satellite radio is apparently free to broadcast—but Mick, who has taken the front passenger seat on the grounds that he's bigger than Tom, decides that something more pleasant is called for. He opts for an eighties station. They endure a few minutes of Hall & Oates and then a song featuring one of those watery saxophone solos, the three men agree, that they never want to hear again so long as they live. Mick presses the button on the satellite radio gadget and they listen to hits from the seventies. The first song up is "Last Dance," by Donna Summer.

Tom recalls the parties he went to in middle school, where "Last Dance" signaled the last dance. Even now, the song gives him an unpleasant feeling of time running out. Next comes Rod Stewart, who Tom has always regarded as a joke. Nevertheless, he is overwhelmed by Rod singing "You Wear It Well." Tom thinks of his sister, who loved that song, and is now in a marriage in Arizona, and is lost to him in all kinds of ways. When the SUV comes to the end of the causeway that leads into Clearwater, Billy Joel begins to sing. Tom has never really warmed to Billy Joel. He voices no protest when Aaron says, "I can't listen to this," and goes back to the rap station, or channel, or program, or whatever it's called on satellite radio.

The three golfers arrive at the Belleview Biltmore Hotel and Spa. Tom has booked rooms at a discount rate offered by Hotels.com that is slightly more expensive, they will discover, than the rate the Belleview Biltmore itself would have offered. There is a moment of slight tension as the men thriftily debate whether or not to make use of the valet parking (three dollars plus tip): on the one hand it's raining; on the other hand there are free regular parking spaces not far from the hotel entrance. What the hell, they decide, and they take the SUV right up to the hotel and delegate Aaron to pay the valet. They don't yet know that they will be charged a parking charge irrespective of whether the valet parks the car for them or not, and that when they check out they will be charged three dollars on top of the six dollars they paid the valet.

The men dump their bags in their rooms and head

straight out to the golf club affiliated with the hotel, which has a course designed by Robert Trent Jones. There is a squabble about golfing handicaps in which Aaron shamelessly pleads for shots. The dominating conversational genre of the weekend is already fixed: amiable bickering with episodes of somewhat willed sunniness.

It is raining softly as they arrive at the first hole. This gives them all the more reason to cut themselves a break and play off the forward tees. Aaron tosses a long white tee in the air to determine the honor. When it lands, it points at Tom. He pulls out the huge driver his wife bought him for Christmas and, after a couple of practice swings, he hits. The ball slices beyond a small hill to the right of the fairway and disappears. Mick says, "I'm not sure Robert Trent Jones is going to reward that."

After nine holes, they stop at the clubhouse to buy lunch. Mick takes the opportunity to tally their strokes out loud, chortling as the totals spurt forward in horrible leaps of six and seven. Nobody has played well. Aaron, who is especially disconsolate about his performance, buys a packet of cigarettes and offers his friends a smoke. "Jesus, why not, it's my fucking fortieth birthday," Tom says. Mick also takes one, although like Tom he is officially, and certainly for all matrimonial purposes, a nonsmoker. The cigarette makes Tom, who during his twenties smoked heavily, unpleasantly woozy, and he resolves not to have any more, a resolution he will break after a triple bogey at the eleventh. They play on, in rain. On the fifteenth green, as he approaches the shadowy hole with three grubby moons clustered around it, Tom allows himself the thought that this uneventful golf course is, at green fees of sixty-nine dollars, insufficiently superior to the New York public courses they play at thirty-five dollars a pop. Still, it was an enjoy-able round, the players eagerly agree in the locker room afterward.

At the pro shop, Aaron asks the two clean-cut young men behind the counter, "What is there to do around here at night?"

"Drink heavily," one of them says.

Aaron says, "I mean, is there anywhere in Clearwater that's kind of interesting? A bar, or someplace to eat?"

The two young guys look at each other with strange animation, and one says to the other, "What do you think?" and the other one, reading his mind, says to the visitors, "Ybor City. It's about an hour from here, back toward the airport. There's a lot of good places round there."

Somebody told Tom, after he'd opted for Tampa on the advice of a golfing friend, that he'd picked the strip club capital of America for his weekend break. There has been no sign of any strip joints on the roads they've taken, and Tom is fairly sure, from the significant tone used by the pro-shop guys, that Ybor City must be where these famous establishments are located. This knowledge fills him with both dread and anticipation: anticipation because, after all, there is the prospect of women removing their clothing; dread, because he really does not want to find himself, turning forty, watching strippers. Just shoot me and bury me now, he thinks.

"An hour away?" Mick says, looking at Tom.

Tom hears himself say, "That's too far."

"Way too far," Aaron says.

The three friends, who have all been thinking the same thing, decide with relief to eat out where they are, in innocent Clearwater.

They return to the hotel. Tom is rooming with Aaron, and Mick is paired with David, whose flight arrives later in the evening. They make arrangements for a car to pick up David at the airport. This is done with the help of the concierge. When they ask her to suggest somewhere to eat, she declares, "Frenchy's, on the beach. You guys will love it." She gets out a photocopied sketch plan of Clearwater and highlights the route to Frenchy's. She says it's a Friday night, and it'll be busy and—this is nice of her to say, because she's no more than thirty—full of "people our age." Tom takes the plan and inspects the bright-yellow trail they must carefully follow, as if to treasure.

Before they go to Frenchy's, however, they relax for an hour. Aaron wants to go to the Jacuzzi—this is a spa, after all—and he asks Tom to join him. Tom, who has neglected to bring swimwear, is unsure; but in the end he follows Aaron down, wearing two pairs of undershorts. They find a spot in a corner of the hot tub where they can stretch out and talk.

Tom says, "You know, Suzanne's grandmother"—Suzanne is Tom's wife—"once worked for Mr. Jacuzzi."

"She knew Jacuzzi? Wow."

"She was his secretary," Tom says. "In California. Or maybe Minnesota. California or Minnesota."

Aaron says, "And how is Suzanne?"

Tom says, "Great, just great." He shifts to let the current massage his upper back. He is glad he has made the effort to come to Florida. "How's it going with you and, ah, Consuela?" Tom is not yet accustomed to uttering this astounding name.

"Oh, fine," Aaron says.

Tom is tempted to put a more penetrating inquiry to Aaron about the latter's new situation—and about marriage and womankind in general. Tom feels his own unhappiness pressing at him, and he judges Aaron to be a man of the world, with a superior sense of its realities, a man who might be able to clue him in on something. For Tom believes that there must be some common knowledge that has been withheld from him, some widely yet selectively disseminated confidence, some trick of living that he, in his slowness and unsophistication, has not yet grasped. Tom thinks that he has already identified one such trick: ambition. It has only recently dawned on him, as the uncertainly merited and somewhat preposterous successes of various acquaintances come to his notice— Tom is an advertising manager at a magazine aimed at the legal services industry—that those who achieve powerful positions are those who have the imagination to desire them. Why wasn't this fact brought to his attention years ago? Why has he been forced to make this discovery on his own? Bothered, he slides forward and lowers his head into the hot water. He stays underwater for a long time, holding his breath. In the aftermath of the immersion—funny how a dip can make you feel better—his need to talk to Aaron has abated. It would be a delicate conversation, anyway, since Aaron's breakup with Annette is less than a year old. Talk about clichés: one evening, Annette returns from a high school reunion in Wisconsin, declares herself to be a new woman and young again, and demands that Aaron leave the house that very night; which, partly out of sheer amazement, he does.

Tom says to his friend, "You know what, I think I'm done here."

"Me too," Aaron says.

They go up to their room. "You got to shower," Aaron says firmly, as if the matter were in issue. "You don't know what's in that Jacuzzi water." As he waits for Aaron to finish up in the bathroom, Tom turns on the TV and channel hops. On the CNN ticker, he catches sight of the fleeing words ". . . Billy Joel, 55 years old."

Tom thinks, Billy Joel, dead? Only a month or so before, he'd seen photographs of Billy—a white blubbery fellow with a graying goatee—in the *Post*. Billy was on some Caribbean island with his new girlfriend, and she was rubbing sun cream onto his back. Where was it, Tobago? Tom can no longer recall. But he is not surprised by the news, because the singer evidently had drinking problems. He recalls some fiasco of a concert with Elton John, where Billy was too drunk to perform.

When Aaron comes out of the shower, Tom says to him, "Billy Joel died."

"No way," Aaron says, rubbing a towel against his head.

"I just saw it on the ticker. Aged fifty-five."

"Jesus," Aaron says mildly. "Billy Joel. We were just listening to him in the car. The Piano Man."

In the shower, Tom takes an interest in his feelings about the dead Joel. He notes, first, that there's something triumphant about the business of lathering shampoo into his scalp: he is here, applying the anti-flake lotion and submitting to a hot adjustable waterfall, and Billy is not. Second, he detects relief, the relief you feel when you reach the end of a roll of toilet tissue, or—he is unwrapping a square of complimentary soap—when you finally throw out a withered nugget of soap. Yes, Billy was like a shrunken old bar of soap. Now that he's gone, the world seems minutely renewed. By the time he steps out of the shower cubicle, Tom is actually whistling.

It's raining more heavily than ever when they drive off in search of Frenchy's. Clearwater, supposedly a civilized place, looms as an aggregate of malls. Aaron and Tom agree with the proposition, muttered by Mick, that there's nothing to do here but shop in the same stores as everyone else and look like everyone else and behave like everybody else. Meanwhile, in spite of their map, they are having trouble finding Frenchy's, and they stop off at a Starbucks to consider their options. Mick and Tom have espressos; Aaron orders a "Venti®"—i.e., gargantuan—decaf soy latte. Tom says, "Venti. They've registered it as a trademark, or whatever."

Aaron says, "Whatever else you do, don't use 'Venti' to describe anything."

"Yeah," Mick says. "Don't use it unless you're looking for Venti trouble."

At last, venturing down an alley that leads to a parking lot, they find Frenchy's. It's a brightly lit place with televisions showing high-school basketball, and loud green plants, and pastels randomly smeared on tabletops and walls and light fixtures. Old people and young patrons mix happily. The men are fat or red-faced or both, the New Yorkers decide to notice, and the single women tend to dress in a style that Mick calls amateur hooker. There are no black people. Aside from one guy with a terrible duck hook on the driving range at the golf club, they haven't seen a black person since they arrived in Florida, not one. A waitress hands them laminated menus. They order beer, calamari, steak, and salad. While the food is being prepared, they step out with their drinks to the porch. The porch overlooks a soundless black void that they must take to be the sea, or the gulf, or the bay. Mick tosses a glittering butt into the darkness. "Venti fucking night," he says.

A little farther down the porch, a kid and his girlfriend are kissing. The girl seems to Tom wasted on this boy, with his little fuzzy mustache. Tom is embarrassed. Of late, this has been his invariable reaction to the sight of a pretty young woman with a boyfriend: that she's wasted on him. As if she would not be wasted on Tom; as if being with Tom would be so terrific. He wonders, not for the first time, how Suzanne puts up with him. Her responsibilities, even more mechanical and overwhelming than his, cause her anxiety and tiredness but not, as far as he can tell, crashing, numbing doubt. Perhaps it is different for women, Tom thinks. Perhaps they are programmed to function more efficiently, more resolutely. But then how to explain Annette and Aaron? Infuriated by the banality and uselessness of this line of thought, Tom goes back inside.

They finish their meal quickly. "Let's get the hell out of here," Aaron says.

At the hotel, they thank the concierge for putting them on to Frenchy's, and go to the bar. They review their golf scores and contentedly wade around in the small financial morass into which their various activities have placed them: they set off the cab fare to LaGuardia against the hotel costs against the airfares against the valet money against the cost of dinner against the golf bets.

A member of the hotel staff approaches. "Mr. Rourke? Telephone message."

The message is from David. David has been caught up

in Chicago and will have to skip the weekend. He sends his apologies.

"Well, that's a shame," Aaron says.

"The fewer the merrier," Mick says.

They go to their rooms. Aaron and Tom undress into T-shirts and boxer shorts and get into bed. Then the hotel phone rings. Aaron picks up. "It's Suzanne," he says. He raises his eyebrows and whispers, "Booty call."

Tom takes the phone. "Hey, darling."

"How's it going?"

"Great. Just great. Although it hasn't stopped raining."

"Good, good. Listen, did you mail that Verizon check yet?"

"Which one? The one for the phone line or the Internet?"

"I don't know. The phone line, I guess."

"I don't think so. Though I certainly put a stamp on it. Why?"

"I can't seem to find it anywhere."

"It was on the desk, wasn't it?"

"That's what I thought. But I don't see it anymore."

Tom glances at Aaron, who is leafing through a magazine. Tom says, "Well, I don't know what to say, honey."

"I just don't want to be late with it, that's all."

Tom takes a breath. Then he says, "OK, sweetie, I wouldn't worry about it. It'll turn up. And if doesn't, big deal, right? What's the worst that could happen? We'll pay it next month."

Suzanne, anxious, is silent. Tom says, "Listen, just assume I mislaid it, OK? You're in the clear, and I've mislaid it, OK? How are the kids?"

"Asleep," Suzanne says. Then she says, "I think I'll call it a day, too."

"Good idea," Tom says. "Call it a day, darling."

He hangs up with a sigh. Aaron says politely, "Lights out?"

The two men lie in their beds in the dark. Then Aaron's voice sounds in the room. "You know, Tom, about this thing with Consuela."

Tom is listening.

"It may seem great, and it is great, of course it is," Aaron says. "But there's no escape, is there? You know what I'm talking about? Whether, I don't know, you're on a beach in Thailand with a bunch of underage hookers or whether you're watching *The Battle of Algiers* with a hot little law professor. Either way it's one damn thing after another. You know what I mean?"

Tom senses that Aaron is warning him about something—putting him on notice of something important. This could be it: one of those inklings he needs. Tom says cautiously, "I guess so."

The two men lie there. "Well, I'm bushed," Aaron says. "Goodnight."

"Goodnight," Tom says.

The next morning they drive off to another golf course with the intention of playing thirty-six holes, although Mick is nervous about whether he will have the stamina to do it. At the first tee, the course starter has a New York accent. He tells them that he worked for many years in Manhattan as a homicide detective. The ex-cop says that he'd thought about retiring to the east coast of Florida but preferred it here on the Gulf on account of there being much less "bustle."

"You know what he means by 'bustle,'" Aaron says, once they are safely out on the first fairway.

Mick says, "Nothing worse than coming all the way down to Florida to find yourself surrounded by more bustle. Not after twenty years of busting uppity bustle."

Only now does Tom figure out that "bustle" is being taken to mean "African-Americans."

They complete thirty-six holes, finishing just as the gray sky empties of light and putts are impossible to read and straying balls, which in daylight stand out in the woods, can no longer be found. They drive back to Clearwater. Every few minutes, it seems, they hit a toll, and there is a pleasant squabble over toll money and who has or has not contributed his share. During the hour-long journey, they listen once again to seventies music; and once again, Billy Joel sings for them. "Hey," Tom is pleased to announce to Mick, "he died yesterday." Billy is singing, "(This Is) My Life," and Mick immediately says, "This *was* my life," and Tom tries to think of something waggish to say about uptown girls and downtown boys, but can't. When the Bee Gees come on, Mick asks, "What's the name of the dead Bee Gee?" and by a process of elimination, and discounting the death of the youngest Gibb brother, who wasn't a Bee Gee, they come up with the name Maurice. "I knew a guy called Maurice Morris," Aaron says, and Tom, eagerly leaning forward from the back seat, tells the story of his childhood friend John Elder, who along with his father was an elder in the church, with the result that the father was known as Elder Elder the elder. "If they moved to Mexico," Mick says, "he'd be El elder Elder Elder." Now they're listening to "Band on the Run" by Paul McCartney and Wings. When Tom tries to make a joke about the Piano Man getting it on with Linda McCartney in heaven, Aaron doesn't like it. "Come on, she was a nice woman," he says seriously. The travelers fall quiet. Tom thinks back to 1980, when he was sixteen, and two girls he knew went to see Billy Joel in concert. Afterward they met him backstage. The girls said that Billy Joel—Jesus, he must have been about thirty-two at the time, though he seemed so ancient—had been very kind and very respectful. Tom thinks about mentioning this incident, about saying something good about Billy Joel.

They take dinner at the hotel. There's no talk of Frenchy's or Ybor City.

The next morning, Sunday, they play one last round on the hotel course, this time off the back tees, and afterward go directly to Tampa Airport. There, Tom is again confronted by the irksome unworldliness that for some reason seems to be overtaking him. He is at the curbside check-in counter when Aaron says to him, "Don't check in here, it costs extra."

"It does?" Tom was not aware of this. The check-in man—a black face, at last—already has his luggage labeled, and silently stands by. When Aaron goes off to join the long line inside, the man says, in a booming theatrical voice, "Sir, just so you know, there is no charge for this service. If you wish to pay a gratuity, that is up to you. But there is no charge."

"I'm not going to worry about it," Tom says with a smile. "Let's do this."

"I just want to be clear on that," the attendant continues. "You don't owe me a dime. You don't have to do anything you don't want to do."

"No, I completely understand. But you'll have no

objection to accepting this"—Tom hands him a five-dollar bill—"as a token of my appreciation?"

"Tokens of appreciation are always welcome," the attendant says. "But I don't expect or ask for anything. No, sir."

"No, no, no," Tom says quickly.

The three friends eat chicken fajitas in an airport restaurant. A final computation of all monies is made, with paper and pencil. Aaron asks for a special dispensation regarding the double payment of the valet, and gets it. They fly to Miami, change planes, and fly home to New York. On this final leg, they are seated together for the first time. As happened on the outward flight, they are starved and dehydrated by American Airlines, which offers them no more than a tiny bag of pretzels and one soft drink for the three-hour journey. To relieve hunger and boredom, they buy five-dollar mini-bottles of Chilean Cabernet Sauvignon, messily split the Sunday *Times,* and make anagrams of a hard-on product—Levitra—that's advertised in huge spreads in the newspaper. Mick, an ad copywriter, barely has to scan the word in order to instantly to come up with *evil rat* and *vile art* and *I travel.* "Fucking Venti," Aaron says in admiration. A single cab zigzags through Brooklyn to their respective homes. Tom is back with his family by nine o'clock.

The next morning, a Monday morning, Tom is on Fifth Avenue, walking to work, when he hears, piping out of the loudspeakers of a department store, none other than Billy Joel—which, given his death, makes perfect sense. He extracts his phone from his breast pocket and calls Suzanne.

"I forgot to tell you," he says. "Did you hear about Billy Joel dying?"

"No. He died?"

"Yeah. On Friday."

"Well, I haven't seen anything about it. Wait a minute." Suzanne, who is already at work, consults people in the office. "No," she says, "nobody's heard anything about it. Are you sure?"

"I saw something on the CNN ticker about Billy Joel, aged fifty-five. I'm assuming there's no other reason for him to be on the news."

Suzanne passes on what Tom has said. He hears indistinct talk followed by his wife's clear peal of laughter. "He didn't die, honey," she says. "He got engaged. To a twenty-two-year-old or a twenty-six-year-old, we're not sure which."

"Oh, right," Tom says. "Jesus, I went through the whole weekend thinking he was dead."

"Well, he isn't," Suzanne says. "Quite the opposite."

Tom continues walking down Fifth Avenue. It's cold. Ice is piled up everywhere. He has twelve days left before he's forty. Tom perceives—as, apprehending the anniversary as a deadline, he begins to walk faster—that he must in the meantime understand, somehow or other, to soap himself with the shriveling world.

Ponchos

◇

When William Mason made a daily habit of eating breakfast in the dark, tunnel-like interior of the Starlight Restaurant, he was thankful that his parents had called him William. William abbreviated to Bill, and Bill, he believed, was a name to stand a fellow in good stead at the Starlight, a twenty-four-hour diner that served men with no-shit, no-flies-on-him names such as Frank and Steve and Champ. But for all the Starlight regulars cared, William discovered, he may as well have been called Mavis. None of them spoke to him, not even after nine months of spending five mornings a week on the same revolving counter-stool, one of a half dozen bolted fast to the ground like every other stick of Starlight furniture, as if (William reflected one January day) the diner were afloat at sea and not grounded in Manhattan, New York.

No sooner had William conceived this notion than he was dissatisfied with it. As he joined the other solo breakfasters at the counter, he devised a more elaborate nautical idea of the Starlight: as a dockside inn frequented by men waiting for their ships to come in—waiting even

as they understood that, for every tattered skiff of ful-
fillment that entered the harbor, there set forth a fleet
laden with new if-onlys, why-oh-whys, and where-is-
she-nows.

Ruminations of this kind were typical of William
Mason, a man so compulsively prone to extravaganzas
of figurative self-absorption that his wife had only the
day before accused him of "living in a fucking private
joke landscape."

"Joke landscape?" William said. He frowned as he
thought about the conceit.

Elisa Ramirez threw a vintage cocktail shaker in the
direction of her husband's head. On the shaker were
inscribed the words:

HAPPY DAYS AT THE CENTURY OF PROGRESS,
CHICAGO.

The cocktail shaker was a multiply commemorative
article. Manufactured as a souvenir of the 1934 Chicago Exposition, it also functioned as a relic of Elisa's
grad-student days at Columbia University. The cocktail
shaker had been the main subject of her dissertation.

Applying Prownian close-reading techniques, Elisa
had unpacked the beverage mixer's sociohistorical content with the same ferocity and magical skill with which
(in William's opinion) she sometimes conjured rabbits of
wrongdoing from the top hat of her husband's ostensibly
blameless conduct. Her contention (as she'd explained
all those years ago to William, a fellow-student on the
point of abandoning a Ph.D. thesis titled *Prufrock, Pale
Ramon, and the Predicaments of Presumption*) was that

the cocktail shaker embodied a false promise of leisure and escape. How could the carefree realm of the aperitif, with its happy hours and drinks parasols, its egg whites and angostura and curaçao and maraschino cherries, its mud in your eye and its bottoms up—how, in the Great Depression, could it represent anything other than a dream world for the vast majority of Americans? Elisa suggested that this cloudcuckoolandishness was captured by the movie-within-the-movie in Woody Allen's *The Purple Rose of Cairo,* in which the character played by the character played by Jeff Daniels—an archaeologist embarking on a "madcap Manhattan weekend"—repeatedly proclaims his intention to consume a cocktail that he never gets around to drinking.

Elisa invited William to her place in West Harlem to watch the movie and see for himself what she was driving at. The young academics took in the bittersweet comedy while mixing eye-openers. Following recipes engraved on the cocktail shaker, they sampled an Old-Fashioned, a Manhattan, and an Alexander. Finally and aptly, they knocked back a Between the Sheets. This intoxicating carnal ritual—noggin and snoggin', as William was pleased to call it—survived, with diminishing vitality, for two years. By the time five years (two of them matrimonial) had passed, the cocktail shaker no longer saw active service. Propped against a pile of cookbooks and gathering a sticky coat of cat's hair and cooking fumes, it functioned (in William's mind) as a totem expressive of the couple's enduring commitment, through the cooped-up years, to each other and to the idea of the Great Love.

As he ducked the whizzing missile, William was alive to the profane dimensions of what was happening. His first thought was to check on the damage suffered by the shaker, which had bounced off a wall with a hollow crash.

"Fuck the shaker!" Elisa shouted clairvoyantly. "This is not about a fucking shaker!"

William straightened with a submissive air. She was right, of course. But he could not refrain from viewing the incident as roughly representational of the problem confronting the couple. The emptiness of the hurled object; the unhappiness of its trajectory; the fruitlessness of its terminus: it all added up to an analogy for their unsuccessful attempts, these last two years, to produce a child.

Then William saw that Elisa was weeping, and, detecting an unspoken invitation, he approached his wife and held her and waited for the storm to pass.

For this was how William apprehended episodes of this kind: as akin to the rains that fall daily on an otherwise sunny and pleasant place. The fertility treatments had given Elisa a decidedly tropical temperament—which was funny, since he was himself (in the non-climatic sense) tropistic. "*Tristes tropiques*," he whispered into Elisa's hair.

But the following morning, even as he took retrospective pleasure from this phrase, he could not help feeling that his grasp of the situation, however figurally attractive, was shaky; and on his way into the city he was pained afresh by the powerful resignation with which Elisa, after she'd untangled him from her, turned to prepare dinner (soup with scallops). Precisely how, William wondered as he emerged from the subway and leaped over a frozen curbside pool, should he take her remark about his private joke landscape? After all, the alternative was to dwell on the bare heath of literalism; the alternative was howl, howl, howl. Could she not see this?

As often happened when his thoughts touched on this question, there entered William's mind the image of the fish roundabout at the San Francisco municipal aquarium, which he'd visited with Elisa's sister and her kids. The fish roundabout consisted of a ring-shaped tank of seawater in which pelagic creatures from San Francisco Bay sped by in a counterclockwise direction. William stood silently in the dark of the viewing area as large and small swimmers orbited him. Gangs of Pacific mackerel and yellowtail jack came around again and again. A solitary stingray, looking harassed and out of place, flapped clumsily into the one-knot current. No sharks, William noted. He contemplated the rush of fish from a metaphysical perspective. These circuiteers were incapable of seeing, let alone comprehending, the nonaquatic dimension in which he stood. Ignorant of the nature and limits of their element, cluelessly and helplessly circumfluent, they went onward, for the entertainment of unimaginable extraneous beings, without the slightest prospect of progress or illumination or salvation. William filled with despair. The fish roundabout was an unimprovable metaphor of the human condition.

The revelation compelled William to abandon his artistic activities, which was to say, his nocturnal attempts to write poems. As a poet, he was animated by mankind's relationship to the spatial and temporal infinities. Since the fish roundabout constituted the last word, or image, on these themes, silence was the only intellectually honest course of action open to him. William toyed briefly with the idea of constructing a fish roundabout of his own and displaying it as an artistic installation, but he lacked the vocational urge and desperation for fame that were necessary to realize such a project. Released from the ambitions of high art, he applied himself more contentedly to his work as a copy editor. His office was on West Twenty-third Street, a hundred yards from the Starlight Restaurant.

"Menu?" said the man behind the counter, George.

"Toasted muffin, extra jelly, decaf black," William said heavily.

Every day George asked William the same question, and every day William gave the same answer. What would have to happen, William wondered, for George to ask "Usual?"

William looked down the counter at three members of this class. Two stools away was Johnny, who had painted the photographic depiction of Ted Williams that hung in a corner of the Starlight. Beyond Johnny was a septuagenarian in a New York Mets jacket—Donnie—and beyond Donnie was another old-timer, whom William knew only as the magician. A thin, desperate-looking man—he made William think of the dying Charles Schulz—the magician always carried a pack of cards in a holster attached to his belt. William had seen him do tricks only once, and they were astonishing. Afterward, when asked how he did it, the magician replied, with noticeable bitterness, "Hard work and practice."

William removed a copy of the *Times* from his otherwise empty computer bag. As he leafed through the newspaper, he listened in on the conversation between the other men.

Donnie and George were mumbling to each other about odds: Donnie was a bookie, and George (who thirty years ago had abandoned his post as a border guard for the Bulgarian army and defected across the Greek frontier) liked to bet. Johnny, meanwhile, was delivering the angry monologue that invariably accompanied his reading of the *New York Post,* a harangue typically directed at one or more of Hillary Clinton, Bill Clinton, Latrell Sprewell, Alec Baldwin, Sean "Puffy" Combs/"P. Diddy," Osama bin Laden, Saddam Hussein, and Tom Daschle, personages who day after day popped up in the pages of the newspaper like maddening fairground targets. William did not hold Johnny's tiresome pronouncements against him because Johnny could be entertaining to an eavesdropper, albeit in a disgustingly frank and self-pitying way. It was Johnny who'd propounded the monkey test: if a woman's enthusiasm for sex was exceeded by her enthusiasm for seeking out a man's pimples, blackheads, overlong mole hairs, dangerous-looking freckles, and pluckable gray hairs—for, in Johnny's words, "picking at you like a fucking monkey"—then it was time to "shut that shit down."

Suppressing a query that had surfaced in his mind—what if one's wife was uninterested in both sex and personal grooming?—William recalled a test he had himself devised: the Ibsen challenge. If a romantically promising other could not name a play by Ibsen or at least display some familiarity with the Ibsen phenomenon, there was no point going any further. William knew or cared very little about Ibsen, but the unexpectedly fierce dismay he'd once been caused by a date's complete ignorance of the literary giant had taught him something very important: he could never fully respect a woman who lacked knowledge of the father of modern drama.

Elisa had known all about Henrik Ibsen. His birthplace, she informed William (who had casually brought up *When We Dead Awaken*), was Skien, the Norwegian town whose name was related to the Old Norse noun that gave us "ski." William felt an internal chute-like movement. This was, he understood, love's falling.

When William finished with the sports section and his toasted muffin, his neighbors became animated. They were talking about the mysterious appearance on their TVs of a free pornography channel. Donnie had been the first to pick up the rogue broadcast. He'd tipped off the magician about it a few days earlier.

It made William uneasy to hear old men giggling about dirty movies.

Johnny was also bothered. "What the fuck's the matter with you guys? How old are you, seventy-five, seventy-seven? And you're still beating off to this shit?"

Donnie jiggled his fist. The magician laughed.

"Let me ask you something," Johnny said. "You still thinking about women like you used to? They still drive you nuts?"

The magician, a discreet man, raised his eyebrows.

Donnie said, "It don't go away."

"Oh boy," Johnny said. "That's just terrific." He had a drooping, graying mustache, thinning black hair, and a colorless and shadow-stained face. He ran his thumbs along the inside of his waistband to release the pressure on his gut. This was a signal that William recognized: Johnny was about to ventilate a theory. "Now hear me out," Johnny said. "You got women's rights, OK? Women suffer because they're exploited like sex objects. OK. We're OK with that. But here's what I want to know: what about men's rights? That's right: men's rights. We're the ones they're bombing with the sex.

We're the ones being targeted here. Right? It's all aimed at us. You can't walk down the street or listen to the radio without somebody pushing tits in your face. You seen what they put on billboards?" Johnny clawed at the air with one hand. "Scratch, scratch, scratch. The magazines, the websites, the cosmetics companies, the women: they're all in on it. They all got us simmering. And there's nothing we can do about it. We're programmed like fucking dogs. We're going to respond whether we like it or not. We're talking millions of years of evolution." Now Johnny's speech had assumed the fluency of outrage. "And it's all about money. Did you ask for porn on your TV? No. But guess what? It's there anyway. Can you not watch it? Course you can't. You gotta watch it. You're a man. You're an animal. See what I'm saying? I don't care if you're the frigging Pope; you were born to jerk off. Right? They're taking our natural instincts, and they're twisting them for profit. We're the victims here. The billion-dollar Viagra industry? The billion-dollar porn industry? That's our fucking billions of dollars."

Donnie winked at the magician.

Johnny said, "Yeah, that's right, wink, you goddamn felon."

Donnie, who did not like to be reminded of his past, took a sip of chamomile tea. Looking at the magician, he said, "You don't fuck around. You fuck around and you get caught? You know what you got coming to you."

Johnny said, "What are you talking about? This isn't about me and Daleen—although as a matter of fact, now that you're bringing it up, as a matter of fact she made no allowance for me being a man. She gave me no leeway at all. One strike, that's all I got. Zero tolerance. That's what I'm talking about. Women don't have the slightest fucking idea what it's like for men. Nobody talks about the struggle we have to go through, every day. There's a conspiracy of silence. Nobody gives us any credit for dealing with the shit we have to deal with. That's right," Johnny said. "We should get credit for all the women we don't sleep with."

The magician and Donnie started laughing as if they were at a comedy show. Donnie said, "Yeah, I'm just fighting them off. I'm a real hero. I should get a medal."

The magician said something under his breath. This started them off again, laughing so hard that Donnie had to get off his stool.

Johnny crumpled his napkin in disgust. "What's the point in discussing anything with you people."

This was the moment when Johnny swung round on his stool and spoke for the first time to William Mason. He said, "So how about it, bud? You with me on this one?"

William was too surprised to immediately respond. Then he said, "I think it's an interesting question."

"Yeah?" Johnny said.

"I have a friend," William said deliberately, "who's an artist—a painter. There isn't anyone with a greater appreciation and understanding of art than my friend."

Johnny said, "I hear you, buddy. I'm an artist myself."

"This friend once told me something that I've always remembered. In a museum, he said, you could be looking at the world's most interesting, most celebrated painting—a Picasso, say, or a Vermeer—but, if an attractive woman stands next to you, she's what you look at. The Vermeer is just a bunch of color and paper."

William sensed that this insight hadn't produced in

his companions, as it had in him, an aesthetic break-through. He elaborated, "His point was that not even a great work of art can compete with the feelings triggered by the everyday spectacle of a woman."

Johnny said, "So you're saying I'm right. You're say-ing that men are programmed to suffer."

"Um, I suppose so," William said. "In a sense."

And it was true, William admitted to himself, that in springtime he was mugged by spasms of longing caused by the appearance of certain women walking down the street. But William could in all honesty commend him-self for the fact that, post-Elisa, these involuntary physi-ological reactions had never turned into temptation. This achievement, William believed, rested on the notion of the Great Love with which he'd consciously—and, so far as he was aware, reciprocally—mythified his relation-ship with Elisa Ramirez. The myth, formalized in due course by marital vows, meant that any threat or adver-sity (even death, William could sometimes bring himself to think) could be withstood by a willfully romantic adjustment of perception. Like Islam or Marxism, the Great Love was an all-embracing narrative that, as Wil-liam pictured it, rooted fast commitment's tree against the wind and rain of erosive time and the odd light-ning bolt of third-party allure. On this last score, Wil-liam was helped by items of empirical self-knowledge: first, that he would take little pleasure in an isolated or treacherous sexual encounter; second, that nothing lib-erated and excited him more "in bed"—he had always found this metonym hilarious—than the profound close-ness and consent that a faithful marriage stimulated, all being well.

But was all well? For some time, his and Elisa's love-making efforts had been marred by procreative effort. The problem wasn't simply the interference of thermometers, ovulation charts, copulation schedules, and ejaculatory precautions. The problem, according to William, was the calamitously teleological nature of the sexual act. To be any good, sex, like art, had to be first and foremost an exploration of pleasure.

When he'd shared this satisfying thought with Elisa, she was in the bathroom, getting ready to go to Hunter College, where she worked as a history professor. She snapped, "What?" with a tone of pure revulsion. This small moment injured and bewildered him. For weeks he visualized Elisa's loveless expression and stung himself with the contempt in her voice. He saw himself as she had at that moment: as a pedantic ("You mean 'finicky'" was the joke William liked to make to people who accused him of being this) and ugly bore. William—a tall, blond man with baggy jowls, a baggy physique, and baggy eyes (Gucci eyes, Elisa used to call them)—had always assumed that, absent clear evidence to the contrary, he was repellent to all women except for Elisa. Now this exception no longer applied. His self-loathing became so acute that one weekend, when Elisa was on the West Coast visiting her parents, he lay down on a mirror and maneuvered his face into positions that yielded grotesque reflections reminiscent, in his mind, of Francis Bacon's squashed visages. His torment had further symptoms. In Elisa's company he found himself very tired and, to her obvious irritation, oddly hard of hearing. He was hampered by a strong sense that his wife was, in substance, submitting to his fleshly trespass for reproductive purposes, and as a result her naked body—that of a small, boyish, dark-haired woman—was horribly emptied of erotic significance. It was only with a lot of eye-shutting and gritty concentration that he was able to do his cyclical coital duty.

After several months, William began to feel better. He'd been depressed and irrational, he decided, and in all likelihood the victim of some chemical imbalance. He did not speak to Elisa about what he'd been through; and she, who during his gloom had been subdued and preoccupied, did not throw him any more looks of detestation.

Around this time, back in the fall, the couple decided to consult a world-famous fertility specialist, a Dr. Nico Hildenberg, whose services happened to be covered by Elisa's health insurance. Hildenberg was a languid, well-groomed man in his forties who looked a lot like the golfer David Duval. He ran a clinic on the Upper East Side that processed huge numbers of patients in furtherance of a vast research project. Immediately after examining Elisa, Hildenberg prescribed a regime of tests and treatments that exposed her to gynecological peering and scraping, to perpetual "blood work," and—just thinking about it made William angry and loving—to injecting herself about fifteen days a month with figure-bloating and mood-disturbing hormones.

William's role was to produce semen samples from time to time. Listening to Johnny's speech about the sexual victimization of men, William remembered that he had an appointment scheduled for later that week. How he dreaded it.

He dreaded, first of all, walking into the build-

ing that announced itself, in huge lettering posted on
its front elevation, as THE SAMUEL P. SCHLOSSBERG
CLINIC FOR REPRODUCTIVE HOPE. This mode of public humiliation, William noticed, seemed to be common
in this corner of Manhattan, where medical facilities
adopted designations that, in trumpeting their benefactors' generosity, were horribly specific and loud about
their patients' diseases and difficulties. William dreaded
the waiting room full of barren couples, but most of all
he dreaded the room where the semen producers waited
for the signal to proceed, as nonchalantly as possible,
to the masturbation chamber. The chamber contained a
sink, hand wipes, soap, lubricant, a pile of pornographic
publications, a video-TV set, and a leatherette chair that
seemed to have been removed from the business class
section of an airplane.

On entering for the first time, William was confused
by the expectations generated by the amenities. Was the
chair compulsory? Should he watch a video? What was
the significance of the lubricant? He was also troubled
by the perennial question of time: if he emerged from
the room after a minute or two, he would be marked
down as a premature ejaculator and erotic pubescent; if
he lingered much longer, he would be suspected of enjoying himself. Setting aside these uncertainties, William
dropped his trousers and got down to the job at hand,
aided not by the available pornography but by imagin-
ing Elisa and himself in historic and fantastic situations
of ardor. (That was the most exciting fantasy: the fantasy of himself as an object of desire.) Just as he reached
the moment of emission, he realized that he was unsure
about exactly what to do with the receptacle he was

holding; and, fumbling and panicking, he watched in horror as his semen—three days' worth, in accordance with the "abstinence instructions"—spat into, and then escaped out of, the downward-tilting glass tube. Almost all of it ended up on his leg. For a minute or two, William sat on the leatherette chair in a state of anguish. A whole month of injections and drugs and anxiety had been wasted. Opening his eyes, he glanced again at the tube and its negligible contents. "Oh, no," he said.

He fastened his belt and placed the useless sample into a compartment in the wall. Overcoming an impulse to emigrate forthwith to a distant island—Micronesian scenes actually flashed through his mind—he wretchedly presented himself to a female laboratory worker. It was decided, after a short, shameful discussion, that William would try to produce a second sample in an hour or two, after he'd "relaxed."

William collected Elisa from the waiting room and went with her to a coffee shop across the street from the clinic. He told her the bad news.

To his amazement, Elisa laughed. "Oh, Will, you're so clumsy. I should have guessed this would happen." She said, "Look, it's not the end of the world. You'll go back in there and do it again, this time properly, and everything will be just fine."

"The quality won't be the same," William said. He added, "I'm not sure that it's going to be that easy. I don't know that I'll be able to make it happen."

"Sure you can," Elisa said. She reached over. William felt the small, warm shock of her grip on his hand.

He shook his head. "It's no fun in there, Elisa. I'm not sure I can face it again."

His wife got up from her seat across the booth and sat down next to him. "Why don't I go in there with you?" she whispered. "Let me help you."

"No way," William said. "Absolutely not. No."

"Why not?" she said. As she stroked his inner thigh, William recalled her astonishing libidinousness during their early months together. It was almost incredible to him, now, that one night in SoHo she'd dropped to her knees on the wet cobbles and he'd been forced, out of embarrassment and fear of arrest, to restrain her from undoing his zipper. "I'm sure it happens a lot," Elisa said, tugging at his earlobe with her teeth. "Nobody's going to mind. Besides, I'd like to be there. It'll make it special."

He saw that she was trying to bring into the world a romantically sustaining event. He said, "No, I can't do that. Stop. Stop that."

Not noticing her husband's anger, she persisted in kneading his thigh with her stout, freckled hand.

"I said stop," he hissed.

"OK, fine," Elisa said. She smiled courageously.

William decided not to say what was on his mind: that this show of passion was too late, and wrong, and certainly fraudulent, that she had at some unidentifiable moment forfeited some right he couldn't immediately name. "I'll take care of it on my own," he said, picking up the menu. "Don't worry about it."

A short while later, William returned to the clinic and, embroiled in a movie about lesbian sex and with no thought of Elisa, successfully produced a sample.

◇

The conversation at the Starlight had picked up again. Now Johnny was telling a story about something he'd seen in a restaurant in his hometown, New Haven. "So this guy came crashing into the joint with blood all over him. He just came barging in through the door and started lurching against the chairs and tables. Everybody started laughing. They thought it was a stunt. They thought he was clowning around with ketchup. His so-called blood was dripping everywhere. It was falling on my shoes, in my beer, in my girlfriend's coffee. He fell to the ground, bang, right by my feet. I saw that he had this gash in his neck, a long, skinny kind of gash, like a mouth." Johnny shook his head. "Just awful. Meanwhile, get this: everybody kept on laughing. The poor son of a bitch was lying there in a pool of blood, fighting for his life, and all he could hear was fucking laughter."

"What happened to him?" George asked.

"I assume he died, George," Johnny said.

"You assume?"

"Well, we didn't want to get mixed up in anything," Johnny said. "We took off."

There was a silence. Then the magician spoke up. "Something happened to me that was almost exactly the same thing. This is almost fifty years ago, now. I was living in Newark. The only reason I'd go into the city was if I was going on a big date. You know: show them the sights, maybe catch a movie, act like a big shot. I was a real Romeo. I had it down pat. Although it got to be confusing, because I couldn't remember which landmark I'd shown to which girl." The magician chuckled. "Anyhow, one day I take this young lady to a fancy place near Times Square. Ruby Silverman. We'd been seeing each other for a good while, and I took her to this restaurant to break it off with her."

"You're going to finish with her in a restaurant?" Johnny said.

"Well, maybe not in the restaurant, but certainly on that date," the magician said. "I figure I'm going to do it with class, because I like this girl a lot, I respect her, and she deserves to be treated right."

"I like your style," Johnny said.

"So we're eating. Suddenly, she puts down her knife and fork and says, 'Stanley, are you going to marry me?' And I say, 'I can't say yes, so you'll have to take that as a no.'"

"Pretty smooth," Johnny said.

"Ruby Silverman. Jesus, I sometimes wonder what became of her."

Johnny said, "So what happened?"

"Sitting next to us is a black man who's having dinner with his two grown-up daughters. He's kind of a heavyset guy. Fat. He's wearing a nice suit, and he has a napkin around his neck so that the spaghetti sauce won't stain his shirt. Can you believe I remember that napkin? Right as I'm telling Ruby it's not going to work out, I hear this shuffling sound. It's this guy, and he's having a heart attack. His face is all swollen and he's kind of bent over the table, very still. But his daughters are just eating their food. They're eating as if nothing has happened. They seem annoyed that their father is having a heart attack. They wish he'd quit having a heart attack and quit embarrassing them."

How alone we are! William thought with anguish. He remembered how Elisa and he had left the coffee shop across from the clinic and gone their separate ways. He watched her walk down the street with her back turned to him. She wore her tasseled leather poncho. Rain was falling, and she held a dark umbrella low over her head. It occurred to William, as he sat in the Starlight, that she had been cloaked in a pluvial poncho, too, what with the umbrella canopy and the tassels of rain dropping from the tips of the umbrella spokes.

The Poltroon Husband

◇

Five years ago we sold the Phoenix house and bought land in Flagstaff and built a house there—our "final abode," I called it. Jayne objected to this designation, but I defended myself with what I termed an "argument from reality"—which was also objected to by Jayne, who said I was using "an argument from being really annoying."

"Are you saying this isn't going to be our final abode?" I said. "And don't talk to me about hospices or nuthouses. You know what I mean. This is the last place you and I will call home. This is our final abode."

I looked up "abode." It refers to a habitual residence, of course; but it derives from an Old English verb meaning "to wait." The expression "abide with me" can be traced back to the same source. An abode is a place of waiting. Waiting for what? Not to be a downer, but I think we all know the answer. When I shared my research with Jayne, she said, "I see that your darkness is somewhat useful to you, but it's a bit intellectually weak." This delighted me.

The final abode is in a wooded, intermittently waterlogged double lot on South San Francisco Street, near the university. The neighborhood was quite ramshackle when we moved in, and to this day it hosts a significant population of indigent men. They come to Flagstaff with good reason, in my opinion: the climate is lovely in this desert oasis seven thousand feet above the sea, and there are good social services, and the townsfolk are kind-hearted, I would claim, although it must be noted that the city only recently decriminalized begging. I took part in the protests against the law. Jayne, whose politics on this issue are the same as mine, was disinclined to man the barricades, so to speak. We, the protesters, chanted slogans and held up placards and marched along Beaver Street, where some of us got into good trouble, to use the catchphrase: we sat down in the middle of the road and symbolically panhandled. I was among those sitting down but not among those randomly arrested and dragged away by the cops, much to Jayne's relief.

Our house, the very clever work of a local architect, consists of five shipping containers raised several feet above the ground. Half of one container functions as a garden office and the other half functions as a covered footbridge over the stream that runs through our land: previously you had to negotiate a pair of old planks. The covered bridge was my idea. It makes me stupidly proud when visitors pause to enjoy the view through the bridge's window: the small brown watercourse, the translucent thicket. How fortunate we were to find this magical overgrown downtown woodland. Road traffic is imperceptible from the house; and when the maples and river birches are in leaf, we cannot be seen by anyone walking by. It is a wonderfully private, precious urban place.

One night, Jayne grabs my wrist. We are in bed.

"Did you hear that?" she says.

"Hear what?"

Jayne is still holding my wrist, though not as tightly as before.

"Shush," she says.

We listen. I am about to declare the all-clear when there's a noise—a kind of thud, as if a person had collided with the sofa.

Jayne and I look at each other. "What was that?" she says. She is whispering.

We listen some more. Another noise: not as loud, but also thud-like.

"It could be a skunk," I say. We have a lot of skunks around here. Skunks are born intruders.

"Is it downstairs?"

It's hard for me to give an answer. Although the house has two stories and numerous dedicated "zones," to use the architect's word, only the bathrooms are *rooms*, that is, spaces enclosed by four walls and a door. Otherwise the house comprises a single acoustical unit. This can be confusing. Often a noise made in one zone will sound as if it emanates from another.

Now there is a sudden louder noise that must be described as a *cough*. Something or someone is either coughing or making a coughing sound. It's definitely coming from inside the house, I think.

"I'd better take a look," I say. A little to my surprise, Jayne doesn't disagree. I turn off my bedside light. "Let's listen again," I say.

For several minutes, Jayne and I sit up in bed in the darkness and the quiet. We don't hear anything. Actually, that's incorrect: we don't hear anything *untoward*.

If you listen hard enough, you always hear something. The susurration of the ceiling fan. The faint roar of the comforter.

"I think it's fine," I finally say.

"What's fine?"

"It was nothing," I say. "We're always hearing noises." That's basically true. Often, at night, a racket of clawed feet on the roof produces the false impression that animals have penetrated the abode.

"Let's call nine-one-one," Jayne says.

I don't have to tell her that our phones are downstairs, in the kitchen, plugged into chargers. I say, "Sweetie, there's no need to worry. Nothing has happened."

"Shouldn't we check?" she says.

What she's really suggesting is that I should check—that the checker should be me. I should get out of bed and go downstairs and find out what is making the noises. My feeling is that this isn't called for. Those noises happened a long time ago, is how I feel about it. I feel that they are historical facts.

Jayne says, "I won't be able to sleep."

I wouldn't say that she says this loudly, but she's definitely no longer speaking in what you'd call a low voice.

Jayne says, "I'll just lie here all night, wondering what those noises are."

What those noises *were*, I want to say. For some reason, I feel very exhausted.

Jayne says, "Honey, it's not safe."

I hear her. She's arguing that, even if we could fall asleep, it would be unsafe to do so in circumstances where we've heard thuds and coughs of an unknown character and origin. I say, "You're right."

I don't move, however. I stay where I am, in bed.

◇

It's important to examine this moment with some care and, above all, to avoid drawing simplistic psychological conclusions. In that moment, which I clearly recall, the following occurred: I was overcome by a *dreamlike inertness*. I was not experiencing fear as such. I have been afraid and I know what it is to be afraid. This wasn't that. This was what I'd call an *oneiric paralysis*.

Thus, I could intuit that my wife was looking at me, yet my own eyes, open but unaccountably immobilized, were directed straight ahead, toward some point in the darkness: I lacked the wherewithal to turn my head and return her look. Her bedside lamp lit up, presumably by her hand. I sensed her climbing out of the bed. She appeared at the foot of the bed. There she was visible to me. She fixed her hair into a bun and put on a dressing gown I didn't know existed. She was as beautiful as ever; that much I could take in. She said, "I'll go down myself."

Here I became most strongly conscious of my incapacitation—because I found myself unable to intervene. But for this incapacity, I would surely have pointed out that she was taking a crazy risk. I would have reminded her that Arizona is teeming with guns and gunmen. I would have proposed an alternative to venturing alone downstairs. In short, I would have stopped her.

To be clear, my inability to speak up wasn't because I'd lost my voice as such. It was because the content of my thoughts amounted to a blank. I was the subject of a *mental whiteout*.

My beloved left the sleeping zone. I heard her footfall as she went down the stairs.

My symptoms improved a little. I found myself able to move my feet over the border of the bed—though no farther. I could not escape a sedentary posture. I *perforce* awaited the sound of whatever next happened.

Which was: a soft utterance. Certainly it was a human voice, or a human-like voice. Then came a pause; then a repetition of the utterance, equally soft; and then what sounded like a responsive utterance. I heard a movement being made, a movement I understood in terms of *clumsiness.* Then came a series of sounds made by bodily movements, it seemed, then another, slightly longer speech episode involving one voice or more than one voice, I couldn't tell for sure. What was being said and being done, and by whom, and in which zone: all of these matters were beyond me. I was on the bed's edge, that is to say, still bedridden. This state of affairs persisted for a period that even in retrospect remains incalculable: soft utterances belonging, it seemed, although I could not be sure, to more than one speaker; pauses; the sounds of movements human or animal; and my own stasis. At any rate, there eventually came a moment when the light in the living zone was switched on; and very soon after that I heard the distinctive exhalation of the refrigerator door being opened, and the splashing, or plashing, of liquid being poured into a glass. Here, my motive powers returned as mysteriously as they had abandoned me. I got to my feet and went down.

Jayne is seated at the kitchen table with a glass of milk. She has taken to drinking milk regularly, for the calcium: one of her greatest fears is that she'll lose bone density and end up stooped, like her mother.

"Good idea," I say, and I pour myself a glass of milk, too, even though my bone density isn't something I lose sleep over. I sit down across the table from her.

Jayne is on her smartphone, scrolling. I wait for her to send a text or make a call, because she doesn't pick up her gadget for any other reason. She keeps scrolling, though, almost as if she's just passing time.

I've never seen her in any kind of dressing gown before. This one has an old-fashioned pattern of brown-and-green tartan. She looks good in it. "I like your dressing gown," I say.

"Thank you," she says. "I thought it might come in useful."

I survey the surroundings. I see nothing amiss or unusual. Nor can I smell anything out of the ordinary.

Jayne finishes her milk. "I think I'll go back to bed now," she says.

"Yes," I say. "It's late." I go up with her.

In the morning, we follow our routine. I make scrambled eggs and coffee for two, we consume the eggs and coffee, and we retire to our respective work zones: I to the garden office, where I do the consultancy stuff that occupies me for about five hours, six days a week; Jayne to the studio, which is her name for the zone of the house dedicated to her printmaking activities. We are both very busy on this particular day and work longer and more intensely than usual, and at midday we separately grab a bite to eat. In the late afternoon, I check in on her.

"How's it going?" I say.

"Good," she says, all vagueness and preoccupation. She is standing at her worktable, her palms black with ink. She wears the green apron I know so well.

I peek over her shoulder. "Very nice," I say.

Jayne does not respond, which is to be expected.

"For tonight, I was thinking steak," I say.

"Yay," Jayne says. She loves steak, if I make it.

So I step out and get the meat and cook it. I open a bottle of red wine. I serve the meat with grilled asparagus and sautéed potatoes.

"You don't like the steak?" I say. Jayne has only eaten a mouthful of it. Otherwise she has finished her food—including two helpings of potatoes.

She says, "I'm not that hungry."

"Not hungry?" I say.

"Maybe I'll have some later."

I say to her, "What happened last night? When you went downstairs."

Jayne says, "You were right. It was nothing."

I say, "I heard voices. I heard you talking to someone."

"You did?" she says.

"You're saying those voices I heard were nothing?"

"You tell me," Jayne says.

"You were there," I say. "I wasn't. You tell me."

"Where were you?" she says. "In bed?" Now she is eating her steak.

I say, "You're hungry now?" I say, "Who were you talking to?"

Jayne says, "Are you sure you weren't dreaming?"

It must be said: I'm furious. "Can I get you anything else?" I say. "A glass of milk?"

I didn't press Jayne further. If there's one thing I'm not, it's an interrogator. I decided to bide my time. Jayne, who is a great one for marital candor and discussion, would open up to me sooner or later. Meanwhile, I held off telling her about my side of things, in particular, the bizarre condition to which I fell victim on that night— a *catastrophic neural stoppage.* My story went hand in hand with her story. I couldn't tell her mine unless she told me hers.

Three months have passed. Neither of us has brought up the subject.

The nocturnal noises have not reoccurred. There have been noises, of course, but none that have caused a disturbance. I may have played a role in this.

It has always been the case that, when Jayne and I call it a day, she goes upstairs while I linger in order to lock up, switch off the lights, perform a visual sweep, and generally satisfy myself that everything is shipshape and we can safely bed down. Lately, however, I have taken to staying downstairs after my patrol, if I can call it that. I sit in my armchair. All the lights have been turned off except for the lamp by the chair, so that I am, in effect, spotlighted, and clearly visible to any visitor. I remain seated for a period that varies between half an hour and a whole hour. I don't do anything. I remain alert. I offer myself for inspection.

"Are you coming up?" Jayne called down when I first began to do this.

"Yes," I answered. "I'm just seeing to a few things."

"OK, well, come up soon," Jayne said. "I miss you."

A short while later, she was at the top of the stairs. "Love, I'm going to go to sleep soon," she said.

"You do that, my darling," I said. "Get yourself some shut-eye. You've worked hard."

"Is that new?" she said.

"It's my dressing gown," I said.

The dressing gown had been delivered that morning. It had bothered me, when I began these vigils, that I lacked appropriate attire. To watchfully occupy a chair was a pursuit that belonged neither to the day nor to the night; neither to the world of action nor to the world of rest. Specifically, I wanted to remove my clothing at day's end and yet not sit downstairs dressed only in pajamas. The solution was to put on a dressing gown.

Shopping for a dressing gown isn't straightforward. Not only is there the danger of ordering a bathrobe by mistake, but there's also the danger of buying something that will make you ridiculous. After a considerable effort of online browsing, I got one made of dark-blue silk. I chose well. I enjoy slipping it on and fastening the sash and—because this, too, has become part of the ritual— wetting and combing my hair so that, unforeseeably, I am more spruce than I've been in years. I'm very much a jeans-and-lumberjack-shirt kind of guy.

"It looks nice on you," Jayne said. As was now the norm, she, too, was wearing her dressing gown. She added, laughing, "In a Hugh Hefner kind of way."

Was this an entirely friendly qualification? I couldn't tell; an unfamiliar opacity clouded Jayne in that moment. And when she got me monogrammed black slippers for my birthday—"To complete the Hef look"—the cloud suddenly returned. Still, I wear the slippers happily. And whenever I finally turn in, Jayne is always awake or half-awake and always rolls over on her side to hold me and always asks, "Is everything OK?" It is, I tell her.

When I'm in my chair, I automatically compare any weird noises to those that disturbed us that night—the thuds, the coughs. The comparison has not yet yielded an echo. I also replay in my mind what I heard when

Jayne went downstairs, which sounded to me like a conversation between Jayne and another person, even though it may have been nothing and certainly came to nothing; and I find myself again looking forward to the day when Jayne will finally reminisce about the incident, and will at last disclose what happened to her during those long moments when I found myself in a *veritable psychic captivity,* a state that I'll finally have the opportunity to describe to her—although it may be, because Jayne is given to worry, that it would be best if I protected her from learning about a biobehavioral ailment of such troubling neurophysiological dimensions. It wouldn't be the first time I've kept something from her. I've never told her that, when she and I first met, I had reached a point in my life when it would comfort me to look around a room and figure out exactly how I might hang myself. Jayne is my rescuer from all of that.

It's quite possible that she has forgotten all about the night of the noises. Certainly, the alternative scenario is very improbable: that hers is a calculated muteness; that she is keeping the facts from me on purpose. It would be most unlike Jayne to do such a thing. She can't abide tactical silences. Moreover, this particular silence would serve no purpose that I can see; therefore it cannot be purposeful.

Meanwhile, I've become quite the expert in what might be called *bionomic audio.* For example, I've learned that the chatter of skunks can resemble the chirping of birds. This sort of knowledge doesn't offer itself on a plate. It requires a physical deed. Several times I've stepped out of the abode, armed only with a flashlight, to investigate a noise. One night, while pursuing a scuttling in the bushes—it could have been a lot of things: the raccoon may be spotted in Flagstaff, and the gray fox, and the feral cat, and certainly the squirrel—I found myself in the middle of the woods without even a flashlight. It's true that a "woods" is a sizeable wooded area and that we're actually concerned with a copse here, but to me it seemed as if I was in the middle of a woods in the middle of the night, even if was only about ten o'clock.

It was very dark. Our block has no streetlights, and the nuisance of light trespass doesn't affect us in the slightest. We have only one next-door neighbor, and her property, hidden by oak trees and brush, has been scrupulously disilluminated in compliance with the dark-skies ordinances for which Flagstaff is so famous. I recently looked into installing motion-detecting security lights around the house, only to immediately fall into a deep, scary pit of outdoor-lighting codes. Jayne was opposed to the very idea. "You'll just light up a bunch of rodents," she said. She also said, "I refuse to live like a poltroon," which made me smile. I love and admire her fiery verbal streak.

A "poltroon," I read, is an "utter coward," which I knew. I didn't know that the word probably descends from the Old Italian *poltrire,* to laze around in bed, from *poltro,* bed. Interesting, I guess.

Where was I? In dark woods. But once my vision has adapted to the absence of light, of man's light, I am in bright woods. It is a paradox: dark skies, precisely because they're untainted by the pollution known as sky glow, are extraordinarily luminous. A strong lunar light penetrates the high black foliage and falls in a crazy silver scatter in the underwood; and it's quite possible that starlight also plays a part in the woods' weird mono-chromatic brilliance, which has a powerfully camouflag-ing effect in that every usually distinct thing, each plant and rock and patch of open ground, appears in a com-mon uniform of sheen and shadow. This must account for the strange feeling of personal invisibility that comes over me. I lean against a tree—and am tree-like. I find myself calmly standing sentry there, part-clad in my mail of moonlight, and doing so in a state of such optical and auditory supervigilance that I perceive, with no trace of a startle reflex, the movements not only of the for-est creatures as they hop and scamper and flit but even, through the blackened chaparral, the distant footsteps of someone walking on San Francisco. When my phone vibrates, it's as if I've pocketed a tremor of the earth.

"Love?" Jayne says. "Love, where are you?"

I inform her.

She says, "The woods? You mean the yard? Are you OK? You've been gone for half an hour."

I turn toward the abode. An upstairs window offers an enchanting rectangle of warm yellow light. Otherwise our abode partakes of the dark and of the woods.

I assure Jayne that all's well. A bit of me would like to say more—would like to let her know about my adven-ture in the silver forest.

"Come inside, love," Jayne says. She sounds worried, as well she might. She is a woman all alone in a house in the woods.

"I'll be right there," I say. "Sit tight. I'm on my way."

Goose

◇

In late September, Robert Daly flies New York–Milan.
He travels alone: his wife, Martha, six months pregnant
with their first child, is holed up at her mother's place
upstate, in Columbia County. Robert is going to the
wedding of Mark Walters, a Dartmouth roommate who
for years has lived in London and is marrying an English
girl with a thrilling name—Electra. Electra's mother is
Italian, hence the Italian wedding. Although he has been
to Europe a number of times, Robert has never visited
Italy. Italy, New York friends tell him, is the most beautiful country in the world.

Robert is happy to find himself in the most beautiful country in the world. He needed a pick-me-up. Life
at the bank has been downright difficult. His solitude
is also a cause of happiness because being alone, these
days, is a harmless form of freedom. But driving out of
Malpensa Airport in his tiny, chariot-like rental car, grip-
ping a stick shift for the first time in years, Robert is frus-
trated. Every time he turns onto a road he believes will
lead him south, he winds up heading in the direction of

the Alps, snow-capped even at this time of year and alto-gether astounding in their abrupt and fearsome immen-sity. Eventually he makes his way onto the autostrada. There, cruising at what he believes to be a fast speed of 120 kilometers per hour, he is constantly menaced by light-flashing cars—with a mysterious invariability, sil-ver cars—and, finally, by a racing pack of motorcyclists costumed in checkered leather outfits. Robert makes way for the zooming harlequins. His place is in the slow lane, between gigantic trucks that frighten him.

He is bound for Siena. He plans a stopover in Florence—according to his New York informants, quite possibly the world's most beautiful city. The road takes him through a mountain range he cannot name. On the far side of the range, at dusk, in a spectacle of almost ridiculous gloriousness, Florence presents itself. Robert takes in the crepuscular rays, the golden mist, the shin-ing agglomeration of domes and rooftops. He thinks, OK, I get it. The temptation briefly pushes at him to skip Florence, to keep going. But down he drives, into the legendary city.

Once there, he is foiled. He passes a full two hours trapped in powerful but sluggish flows of traffic: twice the Duomo comes into view, and twice he is helplessly borne away in slow motion to a district of muddy apart-ment buildings. When at long last he penetrates the city's historic section, he stops at the first hotel he sees because it comes with a courtyard in which he can park, and to find parking is to find peace of mind. The reception-ist shows him a mini room with a mini TV and a mini bathtub. No minibar, however. Robert takes the room anyway, just as he takes the receptionist's plainly careless recommendation of a nearby restaurant. The wine he orders warily and gloomily: this past year, he has barely tasted anything. A sinus affliction got him at the age of thirty-eight and, inhalants and nasal sprays notwithstanding, has left him in an all but odorless world. The affliction does not touch him most keenly in the matter of food. He can no longer smell his wife. He can no longer detect those scents that, as a husband, are his alone to detect.

Dinner over, he wanders in a warm night. It is past ten o'clock. He sees only tourists. To his amazement he cannot find a bar. He winds up, instead, following a sign to the Ponte Vecchio—the name definitely rings a bell—where an Italian guitar player is singing Simon and Garfunkel. Robert thinks, You come all this way, to the world's most beautiful city, and you end up with Simon and Garfunkel. Actually, Robert acknowledges that he would rather listen to a terrible version of "Bridge over Troubled Water" than visit a museum or church. He knows what the latter would entail: an hour or more of waiting in line with chattering art-aficionado-mimickers in order to be confronted with a vaguely familiar Michelangelo or Botticelli or what-have-you that's no better than its postcard reproduction. He leans on the edge of the bridge. Surrounding him are American retirees and self-contained German girls with small bears hanging from their backpacks. Robert gazes at the river, the Arno: it is moonlit and atmospheric and so forth. He gets the Arno.

He walks back to the hotel.

◇

There are two roads to Siena, one scenic and one speedy. Robert takes the scenic one. He clocks the scenery: hills, hill towns, and hillsides that obviously have been cultivated for millennia. So this is Tuscany. It is, Robert thinks, not unlike one of those counties in northern California. At noon he arrives in Siena.

The hotel is in the old city, and the old city, as the wedding instructions warned, is an intricate medieval arrangement of alleys and squares built on a steep gradient. Robert finds parking outside the old city and walks to his hotel. Now what? He tries to eat lunch but cannot: all the restaurants are closed for the afternoon. So for half an hour, he strolls. He has nothing to do until the early evening, when an eve-of-wedding reception will be held. Back in his hotel room, he phones home. Everything is fine, just fine, reports Martha, hanging up before Robert is quite ready for it. He peruses a hotel leaflet about Siena's history. Once upon a time, he reads, Siena was a great banking center. Robert considers how investment banking might have been structured in what was, he presumes, a pre-corporate age, and who the bondholders might have been, and whether their crises were like the one that's happening now. Robert assumes so. Then the leaflet reveals that a plague struck Siena and the city lost its power. He flips to the next page but there's nothing more.

Plague, loss of power, period. Robert is taken aback by this.

On his way to the reception, Robert steps into an Internet café. His intention is to kill time. While checking his e-mail, he is distracted by a headline on his home page:

5,000-Year-Old Skeletons Locked in Eternal Embrace

By coincidence, the story comes out of Italy. In the north, archaeologists have discovered the remains of a man and woman buried for five thousand to six thousand years. The intactness of the teeth indicates that these were young persons. It is apparently a remarkable find, even for professionals who spend their lives finding things of this kind. A Neolithic double burial is very rare, and what's more, the man and woman are hugging: it's unmistakable, states the archaeologist, who says she is very moved. There is a photograph. The youngsters' skeletons lie face-to-face. Each has its arms wrapped around the other skeleton. Undoubtedly the skeletons appear to be a pair.

The question in Robert's mind is whether the couple arranged themselves in this way, or whether their bodies were arranged in this way by others.

There's a second question, asked by the article:

Is there someone you'd like to spend 5,000 years buried with?

There's a Yes tab and a No tab.

Robert floats the cursor across the screen and checks the Yes tab. It hasn't been discussed, but it is logical that Martha and he will lie together, or at least near each other, for the next five thousand years, give or take the few decades of their joint lives.

The welcome party is being held at a splendid old building down the hill. Robert walks there. He is happy to be wearing no socks and brand-new loafers. The last thing Martha did before driving upstate was drag Robert into a shoe store on Madison Avenue. Now you're respectable, she said, handing him the shoe box. The purchase was a weight off her mind, Robert saw, a loose end tied. With the baby just three months away, Martha has been spotting loose ends everywhere: the need for a paint job in the baby's room, the dangerousness of the electricity sockets, the inadequacy of the freezer compartment. Martha is on a tear. In recent weeks she has carried around a checklist and a marker pen that makes a fat, satisfactory stripe when a to-do is done. Robert recently picked up the list and read it with awe. A one-word item earned his closest, most amused, most mystified attention. The word, which had a line drawn through it, was his name.

At the reception, Robert wonders who from the old Dartmouth days will have made the trip. The answer, he discovers, is himself. Either Mark has lost interest in the Dartmouth crowd or vice versa or both. The last possibility is the most likely: mutual loss of interest. After all, Mark has been abroad a long time. Moreover, a year after his first marriage came to an end, Mark gave up his London job as a boutique picker of Russian investments—an undertaking whose huge success registered with Robert only when he heard that Mark was in the habit of rollerblading from his Mayfair flat to his St. James office—and worked mainly in Africa for three years, in some obscure help-the-needy capacity. Consequently, Mark himself became a little obscure, at least to his American circle. Robert guesses that his status as the only present Dartmouthian may be referable to the two-thousand-dollar check he once secretly wrote in support of Mark's African cause. Martha would have thought the donation excessive, particularly given the recipient's reputation as a Mayfair rollerblader.

Whatever: the Dartmouth crowd has not made it over. Pretty much everyone is from London. Robert recognizes that he will need to drink heavily. He has some experience of being the lone American at a gathering of English people.

A couple of vodkas later, his friend appears with his fiancée—his wife, in the eyes of the law, because they submitted to an Italian civil marriage that afternoon. Mark is very happy to see Robert and hugs him, which has never happened before, and introduces him to Electra. Electra falls into the beauty category, with long red hair and long legs that move in almost supernaturally small steps and bring to Robert's mind, for the first and possibly the last time in his life, he thinks, the word "elfin." He remembers how, in one of their few transatlantic communications, Mark had said he'd met a redhead. I need to move fast, lock this down, Mark had said. Well, he's done it, Robert thinks. He is glad for his friend and glad to accept another vodka.

You've got to give the English this much, Robert concedes: they know how to throw a wedding. The Saturday afternoon is brightly sunny, and as he sits in the chartered bus he knows already that the proceedings will be a marvel of invention and poetry and organization.

The venue for the marriage blessing is a manor house on a hilltop ten miles outside Siena. The garden has views of five valleys and a ceremonial arbor. Robert is the first to take a seat among the chairs artfully scattered on the lawn. He puts on his sunglasses and stretches out his legs. He is no longer hung over. He feels, for the first time on this trip, relaxed; and his thoughts run with a little more freedom.

What he thinks is that he may very possibly be the only person here, Walters family excepted, who attended Mark's first wedding, to Jane.

It was held on a dark afternoon, nine years ago, at a church on the Upper East Side veiled in black construction netting. Inside the church, statues of saints and benefactors hovered in little nooks, to grotesque effect. The father of the bride, unwell with cancer, was held up by Jane as they walked up the aisle. He died the following week. Jane died two years later, also of cancer. She was small and dark-haired, altogether different from Electra. Robert remembers the homily at Jane and Mark's wedding, a homily memorable because Mark was one of the first of their crowd to get married (Shit, how old was everybody—twenty-eight? Twenty-nine?) and because the homily itself was so weirdly sermonizing. It concerned what the minister termed "the will to love." The will to love: Robert remembers how he'd felt under assault from this dismal, slippery theme. He'd even taken offense on behalf of the happy couple. Even today, when of course he is able to take a pretty good guess at where that minister was coming from, he's hoping he won't hear any admonitions or life lessons, which nobody believes make any difference to anything and certainly are way too cloudy for a wedding. Give people a break for one fucking day of their lives.

The seats begin to fill up—how middle-aged everybody looks, Robert thinks, even Electra's crowd, in their early thirties—and a young Scottish clergyman wears an expectant, official expression. Mark, a handsome straw hat covering his bald head, nervously makes conversation. Robert limits his greetings to a double thumbs-up. Then Electra makes her entrance, in white, escorted by her father. The blessing ceremony begins. Robert is not really listening. He is dwelling again on Mark's first wedding.

After church, everybody strolled over to a nearby restaurant. When desserts were being served, Robert discreetly checked his phone and saw that he'd received three missed calls, all from the same unknown number. Sneaking out, Robert returned the calls. It turned out they were from the animal hospital where his cat— Buster, formerly the cat of his sister, whose travels made it impossible for her to keep a pet—was undergoing surgery on a blocked intestine. Buster had a history of such blockages. There'd been a hair ball, then a piece of leather, then another hair ball. He'd needed three operations. There was hair-ball medication, of course, but Robert had neglected to give it to Buster. Now there was this new hair ball and this fourth operation.

Robert, a finger plugged into his free ear, spoke to the veterinarian surgeon. He knew this woman from the day before and didn't like her. When examining Buster, she'd remarked that he had fleas and had been sniffy about it. Buster himself had jumped off the examining table and taken an interest in the room. Then he was removed.

Through the roar of the traffic, Robert heard this vet quite animatedly tell him that the operation had gone well, only stating as a kind of afterthought that Buster had reacted badly to the anesthetic and was—Robert had to extract the words from her—in a coma. It was a case of a brief but serious deprivation of oxygen to the brain. Robert found himself unable to speak. He went inside to

Martha, a new girlfriend back then. They left the restaurant immediately and took a short taxi ride to the animal hospital on York Avenue. They were shown into a room. Robert saw a cat stretched out on a table with its eyeballs turned into its head and its mouth stretched open by a tube. Its four legs, strapped to the tabletop, were splayed out in a way that made no sense. The cat looked nothing like Buster. It didn't even look like a cat. The vet offered some clearly dishonest and meaningless statistics about the thing's chances of recovery. She also referred to the expense of keeping it alive. Martha held Robert's hand as he listened to all of this. When she understood that Robert could not speak, she took it upon herself to ask the vet the necessary questions. When the vet again said, The operation was a complete success, Martha said, You know what? We'd appreciate it if you stopped saying that.

The next morning, nothing had changed. The plug was pulled on Buster. There were various options with regard to the remains. Robert decided on the gratis option, namely the garbage. Buster was garbage at this point. Over the next few days, handwritten condolence cards arrived from vets. Bills, too.

On the other hand, this was when Martha had revealed herself to be a rock, and that turned out to be a big deal.

Suddenly everybody stands for a hymn, and Robert can barely get to his feet.

Under God, Mark and Electra make their vows. When the service comes to a close, Robert locates the small packet of rice he noticed earlier, under his seat. He empties the packet into his hand and tosses the grains on Mark and Electra.

◇

Dinner is in the manor house. The names on the place cards are anagrams, and Robert Daly takes the seat set aside for LADY T. BORER. He finds himself between a Colombian and an Indian: evidently, this is the foreigners' table. Robert spends the first course pretending to take an interest in the Indian man's bizarrely forceful opinions about the future of the dollar, the euro, and the yen. (The Indian man calls Robert Roger. Robert begins to correct him, meaning to point out that his anagram name has no "g" in it, but abandons the correction. He thinks, Roger, Robert, whatever.) During the main course he talks to the Colombian woman. They talk about kidnapping insurance, which is, it seems, a necessity in Colombia. These topics are disturbed from time to time with talk of the goose. Apparently there is a goose present at the wedding. The goose lives at the manor house and is socially very sophisticated. The goose is a character. Everybody at Robert's table seems to have a story about the goose.

The speeches start. They are all funny and confident and moving, and Robert, who has witnessed this national facility time and again, wonders if making after-dinner remarks is somehow part of the British educational curriculum. Mark's speech mentions him for having come all the way from New York. None of the speakers mentions Mark's first wife. It is Electra's day.

Night falls. A dance floor has been designated on the flagstones of the terrace, and dancing begins. Here the wedding's one weakness shows itself: the disc jockey is an Italian, and Italians—Robert knows this because of his failed attempts, when driving down from Milan, to find a not-shit radio station—have a tin ear for pop music. The dancers must contend with a mix of Euro hits and hyperbolic Italian ballads. But everybody has a good time, notably the clergyman, who twirls around in a kilt. Robert isn't much of a dancer, but he is happy to hold a constantly replenished drink and look on. Mark joins him for a few minutes and puts an arm on his shoulder. Robert tells Mark how good he's looking. Bob, I feel good, Mark replies. Man, I feel good. Then he bounds onto the dance floor and shimmies up to his wife. The new Mrs. Mark Walters, Robert sees, is a quite remarkable mover. That bodes well, he theorizes, for the bedroom. How did Jane dance? He cannot remember. He didn't really get to know Jane. She parachuted into Mark's life out of nowhere and then disappeared with him to England and then never came back, because she was buried there, in England, even though her family was in Maine.

On his way to the bar, Robert trips and almost falls. The Indian currency expert approaches him like the oldest of friends and refines a point he made earlier about the euro versus the dollar. Robert/Roger nods and nods. Then, interrupting, he says, *Cambio*. This draws a silence from his interlocutor. Italian for "change," Robert says. Maybe it's Spanish, too. Anyhow—*cambio*. Remember that word. And *bureau de change*. Very useful. Fully obnoxious, he gives the expert a farewell pat on the back. Now he will dance.

Robert dances.

When he is done, he picks up a chair and drags it one-handed beyond some bushes until he comes to the edge of the hilltop. He accomplishes this barefoot. He has kicked off his painful new loafers, which lie somewhere on the lawn behind him. He crashes into the chair and drinks from a beer bottle. An incline is detectable a few feet away; beyond that is some kind of drop. Farther out, a single road curves between hills. Every other place is free of human activity and free of human lighting. The hills are very black. There's the matter of the moon, however. The moon is big, circular, ablaze. Robert thinks, This wedding is a masterpiece. They've roped in the fucking moon.

He turns to see if he can glimpse the newlyweds through the bushes. There is no sign of them, indeed almost no sign of the wedding: it seems to have drifted away. He is conscious of the grass under his feet, and he shuffles his feet to feel the grass more intensely. His tactile faculty, at least, is fully operational, so much so that he becomes aware of the bones in his right foot and, phantasmally, of the foot-thumb his most distant ancestors possessed but which vast ages have gradually amputated. He stamps his foot to get rid of the sensation, which is not a new one to him. He thinks that Jane was buried in England, far from home, because she expected that Mark would be buried with her.

He has company. It is the goose. The goose is white, with an orange beak. Robert catches the goose's eye and the goose looks right back. He is all set to dislike the goose but finds he cannot. Actually, he takes a shine to the goose. Hey there, buddy, he says. The goose is still looking at him. The name's Roger.

Robert looks out in the direction of the hills, the valleys, whatever out there has blackened. Well, old buddy, Robert says to the goose.

He looks at the goose. The goose is purely there. Back at dinner, somebody said that the goose thinks it's a dog. No, it doesn't. It doesn't think it's a dog. The goose doesn't think. The goose just is. And what the goose is is goose. But goose is not goose, Robert thinks. Even the goose isn't goose.

Robert cannot look at the goose anymore. The goose is nauseating. He looks away from the goose but he finds he cannot look at anything without thinking that it's all goose, that he is already buried, everything is a burying ground out of which nothing can ever be unburied, he was born buried, the air is just a material of burial, the universe itself is buried, his child is buried in Martha and will come out buried.

Presently the goose is gone.

The wedding has been coming to an end. A while ago the bus started ferrying people back to Siena; now somebody is laughing and shouting, Last bus, everybody, last bus. Robert stands up. For a few seconds, he goes nowhere. Then he walks toward the laughter and the shouts. Somewhere up there are his shoes.

The Mustache in 2010

◇

Social historians will record that in the early twenty-first century the fashion for a clean-shaven face lost its dominance in metropolitan North American bourgeois society. (The no-nonsense goatee-mustache, associated with manliness, had long been, and remained, a very well-liked provincial look.) It was permissible, and often chic, to sport stubble, even in formal settings. A full beard was almost de rigueur for younger white males who wanted to signal that they occupied, or deserved to occupy, a prestigious role in the culture economy. The more elaborate and antiquated the style of the beard, the more credible the signal. Emperor Franz Joseph himself could have wandered the streets without attracting attention. Indeed, it may be anticipated that future commentators will detect, in the whiskered countenances so typical of our epoch, a melancholy identification on the part of young Americans with their complacent and doomed counterparts in Austria-Hungary. This identification was of course ahistorical. The so-called millennials knew next to nothing about the Habsburg Empire, the centenary of whose disappearance approached without their knowledge. Nonetheless, our descendants may well argue, today's America is best understood not by reference to, say, Italy in around 1920, a period of substantive national chaos, but rather by reference to the complex political contradictions that characterized the relatively prosperous Dual Monarchy of a decade earlier, contradictions in many ways comparable to those obtaining in the United States during the abovementioned beard craze, when a vast, apparently stable, multiethnic and multicultural polity depended for its cohesion on a philosophical and legal apparatus comparable, in its old idealism, to the outdated dynastical raison d'être of Austria-Hungary. All of this is by way of introducing the drama of Alexandre Dubuisson's mustache.

A youngish businessman (to be thirty-six in New York City was to be considered on the young side, it will be chronicled), Alex availed himself of the new shaving norm. That is, he shaved only every third Monday morning. To put it another way, he always shaved a three-week-old beard. The growth was black and dense, especially above the upper lip. Almost a quarter of an hour of lathering and cutting was required to get rid of it all. One morning, Alex saw that he had accidentally left himself with Elvis Presley sideburns. This amused him. Thereafter, when he shaved, he subtracted facial hair so as to create a comical residue. The soul patch; the cop stache; muttonchops; the Zappa; the pencil; the chin curtain; the rap industry standard: Alex barbered himself in these and other styles.

There was no question of wearing these designs outdoors. They were private jokes. But before Alex did away with the joke, he stepped out of the bathroom to present himself to his wife, Vivienne Ferguson. Viv always laughed, albeit her laughter would begin with an ironic scream of horror because Alex would sneak into her presence and try to surprise her. This became one of their running gags.

Alex's interest in pranking was somewhat forced on him. A Quebecois, his bilingualism fell just short of the standard required for wittiness in English. The bons mots that came easily to him in Montreal were, in New York, just beyond reach. It left him with a woodenness of personality that was, above all, unjust. The practical jokes mitigated this, as did the adoption of certain postures of droll Gallic dignity. He professed to object to the custom, popular in the under-forties cohort, of removing shoes when entering a home; and when friends invited him and Viv over for dinner he would theatrically bring out a pair of velvet slippers to wear indoors. Viv, who spoke no French, sympathized with her husband. She knew that he actually didn't give a hoot about walking around in socks. He just wanted to take a painful weakness—his alienness—and, by doubling down on it, turn it into a comic strength.

The glance of posterity, if it is acute, will stop at this detail: the sudden and strange rise of the "double down" trope. A term once confined to blackjack tables became, in this period, ubiquitous. Most important, for our purposes, the buzzword described a new and uncannily powerful, one might even say revolutionary, maneuver of political argumentation. In former times, if White had clearly shown that an assertion made by Black was incorrect, Black's options were either to (a) withdraw his assertion, or (b) appear dishonest. Now Black had a third option: he could *double down* on his incorrect assertion, that is, dishonestly reiterate it more forcefully than ever—and yet not appear dishonest. This was because a person who acted in transparently bad faith was, by virtue of the transparency, now deemed to be relatively honest. Also, by doubling down Black would put White in an impossible position. Precisely because White's position was correct, it was not susceptible to being doubled down on. She was therefore stuck with the role of the reasoner rather than of the straightforward liar; necessarily, her good faith remained unclear; and a relative deviousness automatically attached itself to her. Worse still, any attempt by White to contradict Black's double down would make her appear foolish as well as dishonest. That is, White would be perceived to be committing what logicians of the future might well term "the liberal fallacy": arguing on the false, naïve, and finally ridiculous assumption that the laws of thought are applicable to the argument.

So Viv was always on the lookout for a nonverbal diversion for Alex. When the night of the school fundraising auction arrived—they had two boys at elementary school—she made sure they went. It would be an evening of broad, boisterous fun.

The auction took place in the school gymnasium. The ethos of the event was that the parents would get a little drunk and then make bids. There was a silent auction, for the less valuable items; and there was a live auction, conducted by a parent who was a professional auctioneer, for the more valuable or quirky items.

We must be careful, here, to avoid a certain irrelevance. The unsatisfactory acoustics of the event space; the kinds of food prepared by the parents; the auctioneer's strange outfit: such sociological minutiae are not our concern. We are concerned only with the incident that, in due course, gave rise to the mustache that is our subject.

A couple of drinks in, Viv and Alex sat down at the table where they'd spotted their friends Josh and Marie. Marie introduced her parents—Dad and Mom, she called them—and explained that they'd driven all the way from Illinois. Small talk followed.

At a certain point, Dad rested a leg on a chair. He asked if it was known that we all have two anklebones. It was not known. Dad explained that he'd learned this fact when the doctors had put stainless steel screws in his ankle.

Viv saw that he had a tale to tell about his ankle. She asked him about it.

Dad related that he used to be a police officer in Wayne County. He and his partner were called to a domestic altercation. The partner rang the doorbell. A guy came to the door and shot his partner six times through the screen door. Four bullets hit the partner's torso, which was protected by a bulletproof vest, and two hit him lower down. He lived. Meanwhile a ricochet struck Dad in the ankle. That was how come they'd implanted the hardware. It was quite the anatomy lesson, Dad concluded.

Good grief, Viv said. What happened to the guy?

Dad smiled—at Alex. At all times, Viv later recounted, Dad had been addressing her husband.

Viv said, I mean, what happened to the guy who shot you?

Dad, still not looking at Viv, answered, I already said what happened.

Viv began to explain to him that he had not—and

then she stopped. She said, Ah. OK. I get it. You're not going to tell me what happened to the guy.

Dad smiled at Alex again. This smile, Viv would maintain, was one of those man-to-man, isn't-the-little-lady-something smiles of the kind that she hadn't seen in years.

He said, Like I said, I told my story. He gave Alex a wink.

Viv laughed and went to get herself another glass of wine.

The live auction began. Viv and Alex were not planning to take part. At the silent auction, they'd bid sixty dollars for a whisky tasting. Apparently at the whisky tasting you would learn how to "nose" whisky and how to clear your nose by sniffing the back of your hand—interesting stuff like that. They felt confident about their bid. The year before, their friend Krithika had bought this very item for forty dollars.

The auctioneer was expert and hilarious and gave everyone nicknames. After a little while, he offered for sale the evening's most morbid item, as he termed it: the services of an attorney who would write your will. People laughed and booed.

Dad announced that he was going to bid for this item. He knew for a fact that his daughter did not have a will. He was going to fix that right now.

Marie said, Dad, Josh and I can buy our own wills.

Dad raised his hand. Fifty dollars, he shouted.

Someone bid sixty. Dad bid seventy. It went on until Dad bid one thirty-five. There was a hush. Going once, going twice, the auctioneer called.

Viv raised two fingers.

Morticia bids two hundred, the auctioneer said with a cackle. Sir? he said to Dad. Two ten?

Alex whispered to his wife, What are you doing? He didn't have to tell her that they already had a will.

Two ten, bid the retired police officer.

Two twenty, bid the director of an advertising agency specializing in new media.

That's enough, Vivienne, Alex said softly.

Do I have two and a quarter? the auctioneer exclaimed. I do! The gentleman testator bids two and a quarter! Well played, sir!

Until this moment, Viv had fixed her eyes on the auctioneer. She turned toward Dad. Now he was looking at her. She smiled at him. When asked about Dad's expression at this moment, Viv would say that he looked confused.

She heard the auctioneer say, Does Morticia respond?

Viv raised her hand in a fist. Then, dramatically, she showed five fingers. A cheer mixed with gasps went up. A few people clapped.

The auctioneer touched his bow tie. I'm bid five hundred, he said, very calm.

There was no movement from Dad.

Going once, cried the auctioneer with sudden violence. Going twice. He paused. Sold to Mrs. Morticia Addams for five hundred dollars, he shouted, and he banged his little mallet.

Viv went to the podium to collect her certificate. She waved it in the air, to applause. When she got back to the table, she handed the certificate to Dad. That was so much fun, she said.

◇

The next day Alex, hung over, slept in. Viv, also hung over, took the boys to the park. When they returned, Alex was taking a bath.

A little later, she became aware of him standing behind her, a towel around his waist. His wet black hair was slicked diagonally across his forehead. His beard had been shaved except for a dark square beneath his nose.

Viv said, Not funny, Alex.

Alex made no reply. In a further break from his routine—it was a Saturday, after all, not a Monday—he didn't shave off the toothbrush mustache until shortly before he stepped out, a few hours later. It could be said that he'd shaved it off only after he had first doubled down on it.

I learned about all of this at first hand, from Viv, over lunch a few days later. The main theme, from her point of view, was her misbehavior at the auction, about which she felt, she said, horrible shame. Even allowing for the fact that she'd gotten a little wasted, she could not explain what had possessed her to humiliate this basically harmless and nice man from Illinois, whose eye-contact avoidance, it seemed to her in retrospect, had not necessarily been a sign of misogynistic condescension. And even if Dad had been patronizing (and she did think that he had been, in all fairness), surely she could have been a little more sympathetic to a retiree from a part of the country dominated by conservative norms— Let's be honest, Viv said: dominated by backward, borderline evil norms—that were simply not intellectually escapable by him, undeveloped as he was, like so many members of the American proletariat, in the realm of critical thinking.

I had no insights to offer Viv. As a matter of fact, I was

chuckling loudly as she spoke, because she was entertaining me with an anecdote of social catastrophe and
mortification, not asking for my opinion or analysis. As
for the vignette about Alex's mustache, that was purely
laughable. It was his payback for her disgraceful actions
of the night before, and Viv herself felt that she deserved
nothing less than this husbandly retribution, or lesson.
And his pedagogic method was actually typical of him,
and sweetly humorous, too, once you got over the initial
shock and revulsion.

That lunch took place seven years ago. Until quite
recently, it belonged to the plane of the contemporane-
ous—to the foreshortened phenomenal mass by which
we are surrounded as if in a forest. But time slowly
moves us all upward, into the canopy. With every instant
that passes, an imperceptibly changing chronorama dis-
closes itself. The forest floor becomes ever more visible.
All that remains is the problem of seeing what's down
there, in the past.

When I mention to my husband that I find myself
recalling this episode, or rather that it has resurfaced in
my mind with the spontaneity and portentousness of a
dream, he only vaguely remembers the whole affair and
he asks me to repeat the details. When I do, it makes him
laugh all over again—laugh even more than he did the
first time around.

"Good old Viv," he says.

It must be clarified that Viv and I haven't seen much
of each other lately; our friendship, which has always
been deciduous, is passing through a wintry stage. The
reasons for this need not detain us.

I say to him, "It doesn't strike you differently? In retrospect?"

He hums thinkily. "You mean, as some kind of symbol? Some kind of sign of the times?"

That isn't exactly what I mean. "As a clue," I say. Because I don't want to appear odd, or unwell, I don't reveal that I'm spelling it "clew," as in the ball of yarn, as in the labyrinth.

My husband, Jerry, is a very practical guy. For some time he has been urging me to take up meditation. He sees our conversation as an opportunity to again press this idea on me. A dose of mindfulness, he feels, would reduce my stress and do me a lot of good.

Mindfulness, if I've understood it correctly, means paying very, very close attention to the continuance of one's subjectivity. If you do it right, your thoughts circulate before your mind's eye like mounts on a carousel. Finally, the horses and the dragons quietly gallop away.

This is where I must disagree with Jerry—who, by the way, wears stubble. Since when did "meditate," which in my book means to think something over, come to mean its opposite? He is in effect asking me to perform a renunciation.

This word, "renunciation," which in one sense is an antonym of "doubling down," has fallen into relative disuse. According to graphs charting the occurrence of words in published books, "renunciation" was steadily deployed throughout the nineteenth century (in 1813 especially, for some reason); came into vogue in the late 1920s, peaking in 1929; immediately suffered a crash in use; made a comeback in the postwar period, peaking in 1963; and ever since has gone into ever-deepening disfavor.

I say to Jerry, "We can't afford to meditate. This isn't the moment."

He laughs. "Who's this 'we'?"

It's true: the first-person plural usually would refer to me and Jerry. Now it refers to me and some multitude.

So be it. My point is that we must turn our gaze toward Vivienne Ferguson and Alexandre Dubuisson, this married white couple living in New York City, with a special concentration. Certain customary items—the state of their marriage, the particulars of their domestic and professional arrangements, in short the state of the upper-middle-class adventure on which, years before, they jointly embarked—must be, if not disregarded, then at least driven to the periphery of our vision. And I say this as their friend. Do we care that Viv and Alex make thoughtful educational efforts on behalf of their first-born, who faces certain challenges? For our purposes, we don't. Whether Viv and Alex are or aren't sexually contented, to what extent their expectations of personal happiness are being met—these questions cannot be in our scope. Never mind that, not long after the events on which we're focused, Viv will receive the results of a certain blood test and be forced to think in somber terms about her future and the future of her family. We are not concerned with Viv and Alex as such. We cannot be. They interest us only as creatures in the understory of yesteryear.

Here is Jerry's hand, on my shoulder. "Are you OK, my love?"

I touch his hand. We are high up, on the twenty-second floor. We can see across the river. Clouds—clouds without qualities; clouds that are barely events; clouds no different from uncountable predecessors; clouds that will not figure in the history of clouds—are approaching us from Weehawken, from where they always seem to approach. Although it must be that sometimes they approach from the Tappan Zee or from New York Bay or Kips Bay. I'm brushing tears from my eyes, it should be documented.

The Sinking of the *Houston*

◇

When I became a parent of young children I also became a purposeful and relentless opportunist of sleep. In fact sleep functioned as that period's subtle denominator. I found myself capable of taking a nap just about anywhere, even when standing in a subway car or riding an escalator. I wasn't the only one. Out and about, I spotted drowsy or dozing people everywhere; and I realized that a kind of mechanized mass somnambulism is an essential component of modern life; and I gained a better understanding of the siesta and the snooze and the death wish.

Then my three boys grew big—grew from toddling alarmists into wayward urban doofuses neurologically unequipped to perceive the risks incidental to their teenage lives. Several nights a week I lie awake in bed until the front door has sighed shut behind every last one of them. Even then, even once they're all safely home, there are disquieting goings-on. Objects are put in motion, to frightening sonic effect. A creaking cupboard hinge is an SOS. A spoon in a cereal bowl is a tocsin.

The key point is that I no longer have the ability to nap

at will—to recover, in nickels of unconsciousness, a lost hypnotic legacy. A round-the-clock jitteriness prevails.

As a consequence, the concept of *peace and quiet* has assumed an italicized personal importance. Who can say, of course, what "peace and quiet" means? It certainly doesn't denote the experience produced by being by oneself. I can offer only a subjective definition: the state of affairs in which (1) one finds oneself at home; (2) there are people around whom one wants to have around, not least because it means that one doesn't have to worry about where else they might be; (3) one sits in one's armchair; and (4) the people around leave one alone.

The phenomenon of the Dad Chair needs no investigation here. I'll just state that there came a moment when the whole business of taking care of the guys—of their need to be woken up, clothed, fed, transported, coached, cleaned, bedded down, constantly kept safe and constantly captained—altered me. The alteration made me identify with the shipman, working in high and howling winds in the Bay of Biscay, who dreams of the bathtubs of La Rochelle. This led me to buy a black leatherette armchair and to designate it as my haven. I've got to say, it has worked out pretty well.

But of late, the fifteen-year-old, the middle son, has taken to disturbing me. I'll be sitting there, doing stuff on my laptop, when he'll approach and pull off my noise-canceling headphones.

"What is it?" I ask him.

"Have you heard of the Duvaliers?"

"What?"

"The Duvaliers. The dictators of Haiti."

"What about them?"

"There's two Duvaliers," he says. "There's the father

and there's the son. Do you know that they used rape to punish their political opponents?"

"What?"

He says, "They—"

"I don't want to hear about it. I know all about the Duvaliers. They were horrible. I know all about it."

"But, Dad, I'll bet you don't know. There was one time—"

"Stop harassing me!" I shout. "Stop bothering me with this stuff! Leave me alone! I lived through it! I don't want to discuss it!"

He answers, in his mild way, "You didn't exactly live through it. You just heard about it."

I understand that my son is trying to get a precise sense of the world he is about to enter—the wide world. I understand that this can be a difficult process. I understand that it's a good thing that he comes to me with these questions, which do him nothing but credit, and that these are golden moments that must be savored. I understand all that.

Note that my fifteen-year-old is a distinct case but not a special one. His two brothers are the same. Each, in his own way, threatens the peace and the quiet.

"Where is East Timor?" this particular son asks.

"Look it up," I say.

His voice has arrived from his bedroom, where he's lying in his bunk bed, in a T-shirt and tracksuit bottoms and skateboarding socks, reading his phone. Sometimes he'll come out of the bedroom and sit on the arm of my armchair and cast an eye over my screen while he talks. Which is exasperating. What I do online is my business.

He calls out, "Do you know who Charles Taylor is?"

I'm not answering that.

He comes out of the brothers' room, which is what we call the space in which the three boys are cooped up. "He was a guerrilla leader. In Liberia. He had an army made up of children."

"Stop right there," I say.

My son stops where he is, because he thinks I'm telling him that he should stop advancing toward me. From a distance of about three yards he says, "He made the children do some really bad things. Really, really bad things. He made them shoot their own parents. I think Taylor may have been the worst of them all."

I remove my reading glasses and look him in the eye. "*C'est la vie,*" I tell him.

In my book, this is an undervalued maxim. It is related to stoicism—a too-neglected philosophy nowadays—and it's related, emotionally more than logically, to the idea of water under the bridge, which reminds us that the past cannot be rectified. This impossibility applies to the present, too. The present is necessarily beyond rectification. If you think about it, the very notion of rectification makes almost no sense. You could even contend that one's future is water under the bridge.

Anyhow, on a Sunday evening the fifteen-year-old, my second-born, my Secondo, comes home and announces that he's been mugged. I'm in my chair when this occurs. I inspect him, this kid who is nearly six feet tall and forces me onto my toes when I kiss him, which is something I often do, even though it can embarrass him a little.

He seems composed. But he also looks as if he's just been mugged.

"Are you hurt?" I say.

He shakes his head.

"Tell me what happened," I say.

He was skating with friends at LES, the skatepark under the Manhattan Bridge. Then three of them took a train into Brooklyn. They wanted to skate a spot where guys like Tyshawn Jones and Brandon Westgate and Alex Olson had recently filmed some tricks. They overshot their stop. That was when they ran into trouble.

"Which train is this?" I say.

"I don't know. Some train."

In the old days this would have thrown me, would have led me to wonder what kind of knucklehead doesn't know which train he's on. But I've been a father of boys for quite a while.

He likes tea, this son. I've been making him some while he's been talking. He takes the tea.

To repeat: there were three of them—my son plus his two friends. Three young males. They were sitting in the back corner of the subway car. The car was almost empty, it being a Sunday afternoon. There was this dude close by, sitting between the boys and the doors. The dude had a bag. The dude said to them, You want to buy a gun? He opened his bag and showed them the gun. The kids indicated that they didn't want to buy a gun. The dude told the kids to get their wallets out and put them in his bag. He spoke in a low, calm voice. The other passengers, the potential witnesses or interveners or heroes, were quite a ways down the car. They weren't aware of what was happening.

The kids did as they were told. Then the dude told them to show him their phones. They obeyed.

I ask my son for a description of the dude.

My son tells me that he was a black guy, older, maybe about thirty, hard to say how old exactly. He wasn't fat or big or small. He wore a Yankees cap. He had tattoos on his forearms. These were gang markings or prison markings, my son tells me, as if he or his friends would have a clue.

The criminal eyed the three phones. My son's phone was brand-new; his was the one the criminal reached for. The criminal asked my son for his passcode. My son told him. The criminal entered the passcode and changed it. He didn't ask the other boys for their phones. The criminal told my son that he had all of his personal information now and knew where to find him. He said to the three boys, I never want to see you again, understand?

The train came to a stop. The criminal got out.

"He really knew what he was doing," I say.

"Yeah," my son says.

I say, "It would have been crazy to take any chances. You did the right thing."

"Yeah," my son says.

"Don't worry about your phone. We'll get you another one. We may even have insurance to cover that. But we'd need to report it."

"No cops," my son says; and this is when I see that the criminal has frightened him very much, and figures in his mind as a person of great powers.

"OK," I say. I give him a hug and a kiss. "You did well. You handled yourself well, son."

I don't call him "son" very often. It's a big word to say out loud. It's a word I hold back for special occasions.

I don't mention that I have already resolved to find this man and break his fucking legs.

◇

This isn't a fantasy. My phone has an app that tracks my children's phones. Because children are entitled to privacy, I've never used the app before. But this is an exceptional situation.

When I activate the phone-tracker, a map of New York City appears. Three circles—one blue, one green, one orange—correspond to the phones' respective where-abouts. It's a thrilling scene, for some reason.

The stolen phone is the orange one. It's in Brooklyn, at the corner of Saratoga and Pitkin.

There's no question of going out there. That wouldn't be smart. I'm going to bide my time. I'm going to wait for the orange circle to come to my turf. My turf is the triangle made by Times Square and Penn Station and the Port Authority Bus Terminal. Everyone passes through here sooner or later, especially if they're up to no good.

What this means, in practice, is that I spend a lot of time in my chair grimly chortling at my phone. Orange Circle Guy, or O.C.G., thinks he's home free. He has no idea that I'm watching his every move. A lot of the day he's motionless in his Brownsville residence—I know exactly which Amboy Street apartment building he lives in—and typically it's not until the midafternoon that he stirs. He doesn't go very far. He just wanders here and there in his neighborhood, like a little doggie being taken out to make a number one and a number two. Maybe he owns a doggie.

When he catches a subway train, his kinesis assumes a more suspenseful character. The orange circle disap-pears for a period of minutes and then reappears, usually in Downtown Brooklyn or at Fulton Street station in Lower Manhattan. This loser is so predictable. Occasionally the circle vanishes at Saratoga Avenue station and remains undetectable for an hour or two, whereupon it rematerializes at Saratoga Avenue station. In other words, O.C.G. has never surfaced. He has been underground the whole time. From this fact I deduce that these outings have a criminal character: he takes an outbound train in order to rob people on the return journey to Brownsville. It's what he does.

Once, O.C.G. popped up at Penn Station. In a flash, I was out of the apartment. I was a mere block from my destination when I saw that he'd already boarded a train (to Albany, it turned out). That was a near miss. But my day will come.

I can get so caught up in my stakeout that I let my guard down. The son in question says to me, "Do you know what vivisection is?"

"Vivisection?"

"Operating on live animals. As a scientific experiment."

I say, "I don't like where this is going."

"Have you heard of Unit 731?"

"Unit of what?" I say.

He tells me—and this is news to me—that, during the Second World War, the Japanese conducted lethal vivisectional experiments on hundreds of thousands of men, women, and children, most of them Chinese. This took place in a facility known as Unit 731. At the end of the war, the scientist-murderers were secretly granted immunity from prosecution, and even from exposure, by the United States. In exchange, the United States received sole possession of the results of the vivisections. Evidently the data was valuable in the field of biological warfare.

"Yeah," I say. "Not good."

"That actually happened," the boy says.

I say, "I don't know what to tell you."

Which isn't quite true. I know not to tell him, or remind him, that some of the children abducted and militarized by Charles Taylor reportedly not only learned to murder their parents but also to perform vivisections. On encountering a pregnant woman, they were known to bet on the gender of the unborn child and, using a machete, to cut open the mother's womb in order to determine the winner of the bet.

There's a chance, of course, that O.C.G. might not be my guy. It could be a purchaser of the phone. Given everything I've seen and studied, that strikes me as unlikely. No, the bitch has gotten himself a mint phone for his personal use—or so he thinks. Like every criminal, he has overlooked a detail. That kid he threatened and robbed? That kid is my son.

Once, when the boys were little, we all found ourselves in an airport lounge. We were delayed for a few hours. It was nighttime. Volatile colored lights moved in the dark of the windows, and the boys and I spent quite some time looking at them. After a while, the kids began horsing around. They were being boys—being juvenile male humans between the ages of three and six, to be zoological about it. A certain boisterousness and brouhaha characterized their activities. From my seat, I somnolently kept watch on them, breaking things up as needed and rounding up whichever one went astray.

A couple was seated nearby. The man turned to me and said, "Control your children."

Instantly I was one hundred percent awake. I rose to my feet and went over to this man. I pointed my finger an inch or two from his nose. "I'm going to control you," I said.

We didn't hear from him after that.

Now, it's true that the guy must have been close to sixty. He posed no obvious physical threat. It was no big deal to put him in his place. But something deeper was going on, something beyond calculations of relative physical strength. You don't mess with my children. Not when I'm around. I don't care who you are. You don't take one fucking step in their direction.

What I'm getting at is: I have latent paternal powers. It may be said—and in truth it is said, by a whispering imaginary skeptic—that there's no way a fifty-one-year-old man can take down a tattooed career criminal, a hoodlum Moriarty, twenty years his junior. To which I respond: Let's wait and see.

My next-door neighbor is a gentleman by the name of Eduardo. Over the years, he has kept himself to himself. It's said he's of Cuban origin. He communicates mainly by signifiers of goodwill. For example, sometimes he'll take delivery of a package for me and leave it outside my door, which I appreciate. Eduardo's apartment shares plumbing with mine, and if there's a pipe blockage we liaise about turning taps on and off.

Once, I saw a limousine run him down. He was on the crosswalk—he's pushing seventy and has a slow, hobbling gait—when the limo turned straight into him. I ran over and helped Eduardo get up. There was no sign of an injury. My neighbor, I understood, is hard as nails.

On a Friday morning in April, O.C.G. pops up at the Port Authority Bus Terminal. That's only five blocks away. That is squarely in my turf.

I jump to my feet, put on a baseball cap and sunglasses, and dash out. I encounter Eduardo at the elevator.

We smile at each other. When we exit the building, I hold open the door and wait for him to pass through. Then he speaks. "You play baseball?"

He's referring to the bat I'm holding.

I'm going to a meeting, I tell him.

"I'll walk with you," he says. "That OK?"

"Sure," I say. I'm checking my phone. O.C.G. hasn't gone anywhere.

To repeat: Eduardo is a steady walker but a deliberate one. As his escort, I have no choice but to go at his speed. This is a first, I should say. We've never walked together before.

In a second first, Eduardo makes an important-sounding announcement. "Today is the anniversary of the Bay of Pigs."

"The Bay of Pigs? Huh."

The Bay of Pigs, Bunker Hill, Bull Run, the bridge over the River Kwai: Who cares, at this point? Who knows how to care?

"I was sixteen," Eduardo tells me. He tells me he was among the troops on the *Houston*. His best friend there was named Garcilaso. Garcilaso was fifteen years old.

With that he has my ear, even as I keep an eye on my phone.

Eduardo relates that, after his family had fled Cuba, he enrolled at Georgia Tech.

"Wait," I say. "You enrolled at sixteen?"

"Correct," Eduardo says. "At sixteen." He tells

me that it was in Atlanta, at the YMCA, that he was recruited by the counterrevolutionaries. "Everybody else was going," he says. "So I thought, Why not? Let's go." He flew down to Miami to sign up with the CIA. After two weeks of training in the mountain jungles of Guatemala, Eduardo and Garcilaso boarded the *Houston.* They were given ancient Garand rifles. In the absence of helmets, they wore cowboy hats.

One morning, at dawn, Garcilaso and Eduardo sneaked into the captain's quarters. "Garcilaso had heard there were M&M's in there," Eduardo told me. "We look around, and we find the M&M's. At that exact moment, we see the Cuban jets. Flying low, coming straight at us."

He laughs. He's been laughing softly the whole time.

I ask Eduardo if he and Garcilaso got to eat the M&M's. He tells me they did not.

It seems that this is the full extent of his anecdote. Only in response to my questioning does he disclose that the bombing sank the ship. Eduardo had to jump overboard, into the Bay of Pigs, and swim to the shore.

"Anybody die?" I ask.

"Sure," Eduardo says.

We've reached the end of the block. "I'm headed uptown," I say.

Eduardo indicates that he's also headed that way. We set off.

In the morning rush, this bit of Eighth Avenue is barely manageable on foot. The problem is that an almost impenetrable pedestrian mass, discharged by buses from New Jersey and the Times Square subway exits, hurries south in a kind of stampede. The sense of a great flight—of crops put to the torch, of a ruined and shaken hinterland—is only heightened by trains booming underfoot, by the bleeping klaxons of reversing box trucks, by the disorderly shoving of food carts between the stopped cars, and above all by the strangely focusless expressions worn by the oncoming commuters, who seemingly are devoid of ordinary consciousness. It all bodes ill. Either the barbarians are at the gates or we ourselves are the barbarians.

What I'd give for a green and silent lane. What I'd give for a woodland's leopard-skin light.

In short, Eduardo and I can go forward only in starts: we advance a few yards, wait for a gap in the crowd, and advance again. I notice that he's trying to tell me something.

"Say again?" I shout.

An ambulance siren is shrieking. Eduardo waits for the shriek to pass. "I'm going in there, to get a coffee," he says.

It feels natural to follow Eduardo—even though I'm averse to this particular deli, which I know to be a busy, cavernous, impersonal establishment with an offhand staff. When Eduardo sits at the little countertop by the window, I join him but I don't get myself anything to drink. I listen when he tells me that a small group of them, a handful of the survivors of the sinking of the *Houston,* walked for a day and a night through the swamps. On the second day they surrendered to Castro's forces and, en route to Havana, they ran into Che.

"Che Guevara?"

The prisoner-transport vehicle had come to an unexpected halt. Che Guevara and a woman comrade appeared. They examined the prisoners and conferred in French, so as not to be understood. Finally Che said to Eduardo, Who are you, young man? Eduardo answered,

Eduardo Sanchez de Cadenas. Che said, Are you a relation of Captain Cadenas? I have no idea, Eduardo said.

I was relaxed, he tells me. My attitude was, they were going to shoot us or they weren't.

The older prisoners were not so relaxed. Unlike Eduardo, they'd recognized Che. Shut up, kid, they said.

Nobody got shot. The truck drove on. Eduardo never saw Che again.

"What about your friend?" I ask. "What about Garcilaso?"

Eduardo shakes his head—or rather, he moves his head in such a way that I don't know what he's signaling. I'm afraid to know.

Then Eduardo says, "Garcilaso was OK," and by God that's a very beautiful thing to hear.

For a minute or two, we watch the world go by.

"You want another coffee?" I say. "I'm getting myself one."

"I'm OK," Eduardo says. "You don't need to be anywhere?"

Do I need to be anywhere? What kind of question is that? Of course I need to be somewhere. There is no end to the places I need to be.

I buy myself a coffee. Then I regain my stool next to Eduardo.

Tell me more, I want to say to Eduardo, but don't say, because he seems ready to leave. Tell me more about Garcilaso and about how things went well for him.

The stories in this book previously appeared, in slightly different form, in the following publications:

"Pardon Edward Snowden," "The Referees," "The Poltroon Husband," and "The Sinking of the *Houston*" in *The New Yorker* · "The Trusted Traveler," "The World of Cheese," and "The Mustache in 2010" in *Harper's Magazine* · "Promises, Promises" in *The American Scholar*

"Ponchos" was originally published in *Dislocation: Stories from a New Ireland,* edited by Caroline Walsh (New York: Carroll & Graf, 2003) · "The Death of Billy Joel" in *The Faber Book of Best New Irish Short Stories,* edited by David Marcus (London: Faber & Faber, 2007) · "Goose" in *New Irish Short Stories,* edited by Joseph O'Connor (London: Faber & Faber, 2011) · "The Trusted Traveler" also appeared in T*he O. Henry Prize Stories 2017,* edited by Laura Furman (New York: Anchor Books, 2017) · "The Poltroon Husband" in *Tales from a Master's Notebook: Stories Henry James Didn't Write,* edited by Philip Horne (London: Vintage Classics, 2018)

A Note About the Author

Joseph O'Neill is the author of the novels *The Dog, Netherland* (which won the PEN/Faulkner Award for Fiction and the Kerry Group Irish Fiction Award), *The Breezes,* and *This Is the Life;* and of a family history, *Blood-Dark Track.* He teaches at Bard College.

A Note on the Type

The text of this book was set in Sabon, a typeface designed by Jan Tschichold (1902–1974), the well-known German typographer. Designed in 1966 and based on the original designs by Claude Garamond (ca. 1480–1561), Sabon was named for the punch cutter Jacques Sabon, who brought Garamond's matrices to Frankfurt.

Composed by North Market Street Graphics,
Lancaster, Pennsylvania

Printed and bound by Berryville Graphics,
Berryville, Virginia

Designed by M. Kristen Bearse